John Dryden

The Hind and the Panther

John Dryden

The Hind and the Panther

ISBN/EAN: 9783337310684

Printed in Europe, USA, Canada, Australia, Japan

Cover: Foto ©Andreas Hilbeck / pixelio.de

More available books at **www.hansebooks.com**

THE

HIND

AND THE

PANTHER.

A

POEM,

In Three Parts.

—————*Antiquam exquirite matrem.*
Et vera, inceſſu, patuit Dea.———— }Virg.

The Second Edition.

L O N D O N,
Printed for *Jacob Tonſon,* at the *Judges Head* in
Chancery Lane near *Fleetſtreet,* 1687.

READER.

THE Nation is in too high a Ferment, for me to expect either fair War, or even so much as fair Quarter from a Reader of the opposite Party. All Men are engag'd either on this side or that: and tho' Conscience is the common Word, which is given by both, yet if a Writer fall among Enemies, and cannot give the Marks of Their Conscience, he is knock'd down before the Reasons of his own are heard. A Preface, therefore, which is but a bespeaking of Favour, is altogether useless. What I desire the Reader should know concerning me, he will find in the Body of the Poem; if he have but the patience to peruse it. Only this Advertisement let him take before hand, which relates to the Merits of the Cause. No general Characters of Parties, (call 'em either Sects or Churches) can be so fully and exactly drawn, as to Comprehend all the several Members of 'em; at least all such as are receiv'd under that Denomination. For example; there are some of the Church by Law Establish'd, who envy not Liberty of Conscience to Dissenters; as being well satisfied that, according to their own Principles, they ought not to persecute them. Yet these, by reason of their fewness, I could not distinguish from the Numbers of the rest with whom they are Embodied in one common Name: On the other side there are many of our Sects, and more indeed then I could reasonably have hop'd, who have withdrawn themselves from the Communion of the Panther; and embrac'd this Gracious Indulgence of His Majesty in point of Toleration. But neither to the one nor the other of these is this Satyr any way intended: 'tis aim'd only at the refractory and disobedient on either side. For those who are come over to the Royal Party are consequently suppos'd to be out of Gunshot. Our Physicians have observ'd, that in Process of Time, some Diseases have abated

of

To the Reader.

of their Virulence, and have in a manner worn out their Malignity, fo as to be no longer Mortal: and why may not I fuppofe the fame concerning fome of thofe who have formerly be n Enemies to Kingly Government, As well as Catholick Religion? I hope they have now another Notion of both, as having found, by Comfortable Experience, that the Doctrine of Perfecution is far from being an Article of our Faith.

'Tis not for any Private Man to Cenfure the Proceedings of a Foreign Prince: but, without fufpicion of Flattery, I may praife our own, who has taken contrary Meafures, and thofe more fuitable to the Spirit of Chriftianity. Some of the Diffenters in their Addreffes to His Majefty have faid That he has reftor'd God to his Empire over Conscience: *I Confefs I dare not ftretch the Figure to fo great a boldnefs: but I may fafely fay, that Confcience is the Royalty and Prerogative of every Private man. He is abfolute in his own Breaft, and accountable to no Earthly Power, for that which paffes only betwixt God and Him. Thofe who are driven into the Fold are, generally fpeaking, rather made Hypocrites then Converts.*

This Indulgence being granted to all the Sects, it ought in reafon to be expected, that they should both receive it, and receive it thankfully. For at this time of day to refufe the Benefit, and adhere to thofe whom they have efteem'd their Perfecutors, what is it elfe, but publickly to own that they fuffer'd not before for Confcience fake; but only out of Pride and Obftinacy to feparate from a Church for thofe Impofitions, which they now judge may be lawfully obey'd? After they have fo long contended for their Claffical Ordination, (not to fpeak of Rites and Ceremonies) will they at length fubmit to an Epifcopal? if they can go fo far out of Complaifance to their old Enemies, methinks a little reafon should perfwade 'em to take another ftep, and fee whether that wou'd lead 'em.

Of the receiving this Toleration thankfully, I shall fay no more, than that they ought, and I doubt not they will confider from what hands they receiv'd it. 'Tis not from a Cyrus, *a Heathen Prince, and a Foreigner, but from a Chriftian King, their Native Sovereign: who expects a Return in* Specie *from them; that the Kindnefs which He has Gracioufly shown them, may be retaliated on thofe of his own perfwafion.*

As

To the Reader.

As for the Poem in general, I will only thus far satisfie the Reader: *That it was neither impos'd on me, nor so much as the Subject given me by any man. It was written during the last Winter and the beginning of this Spring; though with long interruptions of ill health, and other hindrances. About a Fortnight before I had finish'd it, His Majesties Declaration for Liberty of Conscience came abroad : which,if I had so soon expected, I might have spar'd my self the labour of writing many things which are contain'd in the third part of it. But I was always in some hope, that the Church of* England *might have been perswaded to have taken off the* Penal Lawes *and the* Test, *which was one Design of the Poem, when I propos'd to my self the writing of it.*

'Tis evident that some part of it was only occasion.l , and not first intended. I mean that defence of my self, to which every honest man is bound, when he is injuriously attacqu'd in Print : and I refer my self to the judgment of those who have read the Answer to the Defence of the late Kings Papers, *and that of the* Dutchess, (*in which last I was concerned*) *how charitably I have been represented there. I am now inform'd both of the Author and Supervisers of his Pamphlet : and will reply when I think he can affront me : for I am of* Socrate's *Opinion that all Creatures cannot. In the mean time let him consider, whether he deserv'd not a more severe reprehension then I gave him formerly ; for using so little respect to the Memory of those whom he pretended to answer : and, at his leisure look out for some Original Treatise of Humility,written by any Protestant in English,* (*I believe I may say in any other Tongue :*) *for the magnified Piece of* Duncomb *on that Subject,which either he must mean,or none, and with which another of his Fellows has upbraided me,was Translated from the Spanish of* Rodriguez: *tho' with the Omission of the* 17th,*the* 24th,*the* 25th, *and the last Chapter,which will be found in comparing of the Books.*

He would have insinuated to the World that Her late Highness died not a Roman Catholick: *He declares himself to be now satisfied to the contrary ; in which he has giv'n up the Cause: for matter of Fact was the Principal Debate betwixt us. In the mean time he would dispute the Motives of her Change : how prepostrously let all men judge, when he seem'd to deny the Subject of the Controversy , the Change it self. And because I would not take up this ridiculous Challenge, he tells the World I cannot argue: but he may as well infer that a Catholick can*

110-

To the Reader.

not faft, becaufe he will not take up the Cudgels againft Mrs. James, to confute the Proteftant Religion.

I have but one word more to fay concerning the Poem as fuch, and abftracting from the Matters either Religious or Civil which are handled in it. The firft Part, confifting moft in general Characters and Narration, I have endeavour'd to raife, and give it the Majeftick Turn of Heroick Poefie. The fecond, being Matter of Difpute, and chiefly concerning Church Authority, I was oblig'd to make as plain and perfpicuous a: poffibly I cou'd : yet not wholly neglecting the Numbers; though I had not frequent occafions for the Magnificence of Verfe. The third, which has more of the Nature of Domeftick Converfation, is, or ought to be mere free and familiar than the two former.

There are in it two Epifodes, *or* Fables, *which are interwoven with the main Defign; fo that they are properly parts of it, though they are alfo diftinct Stories of themfelves. In both of thefe I have made ufe of the Common Places of* Satyr, *whether true or falfe, which are urg'd by the Members of the one Church againft the other. At which I hope no Reader of either Party will be fcandaliz'd; becaufe they are not of my Invention : but as old to my knowledge, as the Times of* Boccace *and* Chawcer *on the one fide, and as thofe of the Reformation on the other.*

THE
HIND
AND THE
PANTHER.

A Milk white *Hind*, immortal and unchang'd,
Fed on the lawns, and in the foreſt rang'd;
Without unſpotted, innocent within,
She fear'd no danger, for ſhe knew no ſin.
Yet had ſhe oft been chas'd with horns and hounds,
And Scythian ſhafts; and many winged wounds

Aim'd

Aim'd at Her heart; was often forc'd to fly,
And doom'd to death, though fated not to dy.

Not fo her young; for their unequal line
Was Heroe's make, half humane, half divine.
Their earthly mold obnoxious was to fate,
Th' immortal part affum'd immortal ftate.
Of thefe a flaughtered army lay in bloud,
Extended o'er the *Caledonian* wood;
Their native walk; whofe vocal bloud arofe,
And cry'd for pardon on their perjur'd foes;
Their fate was fruitful, and the fanguin feed
Endu'd with fouls, encreas'd the facred breed.
So Captive *Ifrael* multiply'd in chains,
A numerous Exile; and enjoy'd her pains.
With grief and gladnefs mixt, their mother view'd
Her martyr'd offspring, and their race renew'd;
Their corps to perifh, but their kind to laft,
So much the deathlefs plant the dying fruit furpafs'd.

Panting

Panting and penfive now fhe rang'd alone,
And wander'd in the kingdoms, once Her own.
The common Hunt, though from their rage reftrain'd
By fov'reign pow'r, her company difdain'd :
Grin'd as They pafs'd, and with a glaring eye
Gave gloomy figns of fecret enmity.
'Tis true, fhe bounded by, and trip'd fo light
They had not time to take a fteady fight.
For truth has fuch a face and fuch a meen
As to be lov'd needs only to be feen.

The bloudy *Bear* an *Independent* beaft,
Unlick'd to form, in groans her hate exprefs'd.
Among the timorous kind the *Quaking Hare*
Profefs'd neutrality, but would not fwear.
Next her the *Buffoon Ape*, as Atheifts ufe,
Mimick'd all Sects, and had his own to chufe :
Still when the Lyon look'd, his knees he bent,
And pay'd at Church a Courtier's Complement.

The

The briſtl'd *Baptiſt Boar,* impure as He,
(But whitn'd with the foam of ſanctity)
With fat pollutions fill'd the ſacred place,
And mountains levell'd in his furious race,
So firſt rebellion founded was in grace.
But ſince the mighty ravage which he made
In *German* Foreſts, had his guilt betrayd',
With broken tusks, and with a borrow'd name
He ſhun'd the vengeance, and conceal'd the ſhame;
So lurk'd in Sects unſeen.   With greater guile
Falſe *Reynard* fed on conſecrated ſpoil :
The gracelefs beaſt by *Athanaſius* firſt
Was chas'd from *Nice* ; then by *Socinus* nurs'd
His impious race their blaſphemy renew'd,
And natures King through natures opticks view'd.
Revers'd they view'd him leſſen'd to their eye,
Nor in an Infant could a God deſcry :
New ſwarming Sects to this obliquely tend,
Hence they began, and here they all will end, .

What

What weight of antient witnefs can prevail

If private reafon hold the publick fcale ?

But, gratious God, how well doft thou provide

For erring judgments an unerring Guide ?

Thy throne is darknefs in th' abyfs of light,

A blaze of glory that forbids the fight ;

O teach me to believe Thee thus conceal'd,

And fearch no farther than thy felf reveal'd ;

But her alone for my Directour take.

Whom thou haft promis'd never to forfake !

My thoughtlefs youth was wing'd with vain defires,

My manhood, long mifled by waandring fires,

Follow'd falfe lights ; and when their glimps was gone,

My pride ftruck out new fparkles of her own.

Such was I, fuch by nature ftill I am,

Be thine the glory, and be mine the fhame.

Good life be now my task : my doubts are done,

(What more could fright my faith, than Three in One ?)

Can :

Can I believe eternal God could lye

Difguis'd in mortal mold and infancy?

That the great maker of the world could dye?

And after that, truft my imperfect fenfe

Which calls in queftion his omnipotence?

Can I my reafon to my faith compell,

And fhall my fight, and touch, and tafte rebell?

Superiour faculties are fet afide,

Shall their fubfervient organs be my guide?

Then let the moon ufurp the rule of day,

And winking tapers fhew the fun his way;

For what my fenfes can themfelves perceive

I need no revelation to believe.

Can they who fay the Hoft fhould be defcry'd

By fenfe, define a body glorify'd?

Impaffible, and penetrating parts?

Let them declare by what myfterious arts

He fhot that body through th' oppofing might

Of bolts and barrs impervious to the light,

And ftood before his train confefs'd in one.

For fince thus wondroufly he pafs'd, 'tis plain
One fingle place two bodies did contain,
And fure the fame Omnipotence as well
Can make one body in more places dwell.
Let reafon then at Her own quarry fly,
But how can finite grafp Infinity ?

'Tis urg'd again that faith did firft commence
By miracles, which are appeals to fenfe ,
And thence concluded that our fenfe muft be
The motive ftill of credibility.
For latter ages muft on former wait,
And what began belief , muft propagate:

But winnow well this thought, and you fhall find,
'Tis light as chaff that flies before the wind.
Were all thofe wonders wrought by pow'r divine
As means or ends of fome more deep defign ?

N,

Moſt ſure as means, whoſe end was this alone,

To prove the god-head of th' eternal Son.

God thus aſſerted : man is to believe

Beyond what ſenſe and reaſon can conceive.

And for myſterious things of faith rely

On the Proponent, heav'ns authority.

If then our faith we for our guide admit,

Vain is the farther ſearch of human wit,

As when the building gains a ſurer ſtay,

We take th' unuſeful ſcaffolding away :

Reaſon by ſenſe no more can underſtand,

The game is play'd into another hand.

Why chuſe we then like *Bilanders* to creep

Along the coaſt, and land in view to keep,

When ſafely we may launch into the deep ?

In the ſame veſſel which our Saviour bore

Himſelf the Pilot, let us leave the ſhoar,

And with a better guide a better world explore.

Could He his god-head veil with fleſh and bloud

And not veil theſe again to be our food ?

His grace in both is equal in extent,

The firſt affords us life, the ſecond nouriſhment.

And if he can, why all this frantick pain

To conſtrue what his cleareſt words contain,

And make a riddle what He made ſo plain?

To take up half on truſt, and half to try,

Name it not faith, but bungling biggottry.

Both knave and fool the Merchant we may call

To pay great ſumms, and to compound the ſmall.

(for all?

For who wou'd break with heav'n, and wou'd not break?

Reſt then, my ſoul, from endleſs anguiſh freed;

Nor ſciences thy guide, nor ſenſe thy creed.

Faith is the beſt enſurer of thy bliſs;

The Bank above muſt fail before the venture miſs.

But heav'n and heav'n-born faith are far from Thee

Thou firſt Apoſtate to Divinity.

Unkennel'd range in thy *Polonian* Plains;

A fiercer foe th' infatiate *Wolf* remains.

C

Too boaftful *Britain* pleafe thy felf no more,
That beafts of prey are banifh'd from thy fhoar :
The *Bear*, the *Boar*, and every falvage name,
Wild in effect, though in appearance tame,
Lay wafte thy woods, deftroy thy blifsfull bow'r,
And muzl'd though they feem, the mutes devour.
More haughty than the reft the *wolfifh* race,
Appear with belly Gaunt, and famifh'd face:
Never was fo deform'd a beaft of Grace.
His ragged tail betwixt his leggs he wears
Clofe clap'd for fhame, but his rough creft he rears,
And pricks up his predeftinating ears.
His wild diforder'd walk, his hagger'd eyes,
Did all the beftial citizens furprize.
Though fear'd and hated, yet he rul'd awhile
As Captain or Companion of the fpoil.
Full many a year his hatefull head had been
For tribute paid, nor fince in *Cambria* feen :

The

The laſt of all the Litter ſcap'd by chance,
And from *Geneva* firſt infeſted *France*.
Some Authors thus his Pedigree will trace,
But others write him of an upſtart Race :
Becauſe of *Wickliff*'s Brood no mark he brings
But his innate Antipathy to Kings.
Theſe laſt deduce him from th' *Helvetian* kind
Who near the *Leman lake* his Conſort lin'd.
That fi'ry *Zuynglius* firſt th' Affection bred,
And meagre *Calvin* bleſt the Nuptial Bed
In *Iſrael* ſome believe him whelp'd long ſince,
When the proud *Sanhedrim* oppres'd the Prince,   *Vid. Pref.*
                                                    to   Heyl.
Or, ſince he will be *Jew*, derive him high'r   *Hiſt. of*
                                                    Presb.
When *Corah* with his Brethren did conſpire,

From *Moyſes* Hand the Sov'reign ſway to wreſt,
And *Aaron* of his Ephod to deveſt :
Till opening Earth made way for all to paſs,
And cou'd not bear the Burd'n of a *claſs*.
The *Fox* and he came ſhuffl'd in the Dark,
If ever they were ſtow'd in *Noah*'s Ark :

Perhaps not made; for all their barking train
The Dog (a common species) will contain.
And some wild curs, who from their masters ran,
Abhorring the supremacy of man,
In woods and caves the rebel-race began.

O happy pair, how well have you encreas'd,
What ills in Church and State have you redress'd !
With Teeth untry'd, and rudiments of Claws
Your first essay was on your native Laws :
Those having torn with Ease, and trampl'd down,
Your Fangs you fasten'd on the miter'd Crown,
And freed from God and Monarchy your Town.
What though your native kennel still be small
Bounded betwixt a Puddle and a Wall,
Yet your Victorious Colonies are sent
Where the North Ocean girds the Continent.
Quickned with fire below your Monsters Breed,
In Fenny *Holland* and in fruitful *Tweed.*

And

And like the firſt the laſt effects to be

Drawn to the dreggs of a Democracy.

As, where in Fields the fairy rounds are ſeen,

A rank ſow'r herbage riſes on the Green ;

So, ſpringing where theſe mid-night Elves advance,

Rebellion Prints the Foot-ſteps of the Dance.

Such are their Doctrines, ſuch contempt they ſhow

To Heaven above, and to their Prince below,

As none but Traytors and Blaſphemers know.

God, like the Tyrant of the Skies is plac'd;

And Kings, like-ſlaves, beneath the Croud debas'd.

So fulſome is their food, that Flocks refuſe

To bite ; and only Dogs for Phyſick uſe.

As, where the Lightning runs along the Ground,

No husbandry can heal the blaſting Wound;

Nor bladed Graſs, nor bearded Corn ſucceeds,

But Scales of Scurf, and Putrefaction breeds :

Such Warrs, ſuch Waſte, ſuch fiery tracks of Dearth

Their Zeal has left, and ſuch a teemleſs Earth.

But as the Poifons of the deadlieft kind
Are to their own unhappy Coafts confin'd,
As only *Indian* Shades of fight deprive,
And Magick Plants will but in *Colchos* thrive;
So Presby'try and Peftilential *Zeal*
Can only flourifh in a Common-weal.

From *Celtique* Woods is chas'd the *wolfifh* Crew;
But ah! fome Pity e'en to Brutes is due,
Their native Walks, methinks, they might enjoy
Curb'd of their native Malice to deftroy.
Of all the Tyrannies on humane kind
The worft is that which Perfecutes the mind.
Let us but weigh at what offence we ftrike,
'Tis but becaufe we cannot think alike.
In punifhing of this, we overthrow
The Laws of Nations and of Nature too.

Beafts are the Subjects of Tyrannick fway,
Where ftill the ftronger on the weaker Prey.

Man

Man only of a fofter mold is made ;
Not for his Fellows ruine, but their Aid.
Created kind, beneficent and free,
The noble Image of the Deity.

One Portion of informing Fire was giv'n
To Brutes, th' Inferiour Family of Heav'n:
The Sm ith Divine, as with a carelefs Beat,
Struck out the mute Creation at a Heat :
But when arriv'd at laft to humane Race,
The Godhead took a deep confid'ring fpace :
And, to diftinguifh Man from all the reft,
Unlock'd the facred Treafures of his Breaft :
And Mercy mixt with reafon did impart ;
One to his Head, the other to his Heart :
Reafon to Rule, but Mercy to forgive :
The firft is Law, the laft Prerogative.
And like his Mind his outward form appear'd
When iffuing Naked, to the wondring Herd,
He charm'd their Eyes, and for they lov'd, they fear'd.

Not

Not arm'd with horns of arbitrary might,
Or Claws to feize their furry fpoils in Fight,
Or with increafe of Feet, t'o'ertake 'em in their flight.
Of eafie fhape, and pliant ev'ry way;
Confeffing ftill the foftnefs of his Clay,
And kind as Kings upon their Coronation-Day:
With open Hands, and with extended fpace
Of Arms to fatisfy a large embrace.
Thus kneaded up with Milk, the new made Man
His Kingdom o'er his Kindred world began:
Till Knowledg mif-apply'd, mif-underftood,
And pride of Empire four'd his Balmy Blood.
Then, firft rebelling, his own ftamp he coins;
The Murth'rer *Cain* was latent in his Loins
And Blood began its firft and loudeft Cry
For diff'ring worfhip of the Deity.
Thus perfecution rofe, and farther Space
Produc'd the mighty hunter of his Race.
Not fo the bleffed *Pan* his flock encreas'd;
Content to fold 'em from the famifh'd Beaft:

Mild

Mild were his laws the Sheep and harmlefs Hind
Were never of the perfecuting kind.
Such pity now the pious Paftor fhows,
Such mercy from the *Britifh* Lyon flows,
That both provide protection for their foes.

Oh happy Regions, *Italy* and *Spain*,
Which never did thofe monfters entertain!
The *Wolfe*, the *Bear*, the *Boar*, can there advance
No native claim of juft inheritance.
And felf-preferving laws, fevere in fhow,
May guard their fences from th' invading foe.
Where birth has plac'd 'em let 'em fafely fhare
The common benefit of vital air.
Themfelves unharmful, let them live unharm'd ;
Their jaws difabl'd, and their claws difarm'd :
Here, only in nocturnal howlings bold,
They dare not feize the Hind nor leap the fold.
More pow'rful, and as vigilant as they,
The *Lyon* awfully forbids the prey.

D   · Their

Their rage reprefs'd, though pinch'd with famine fore,
They ftand aloof, and tremble at his roar;
Much is their hunger, but their fear is more.

    Thefe are the chief; to number o'er the reft,
And ftand, like *Adam*, naming ev'ry beaft,
Were weary work; nor will the Mufe defcribe
A flimy-born and fun-begotten Tribe :
Who, far from fteeples and their facred found,
In fields their fullen conventicles found :
Thefe grofs, half animated lumps I leave;
Nor can I think what thoughts they can conceive.
But if they think at all, 'tis fure no high'r.
Than matter, put in motion, may afpire.
Souls that can fcarce ferment their mafs of clay;
So droffy, fo divifible are They,
As wou'd but ferve pure bodies for allay :
Such fouls as *Shards* produce, fuch beetle things,
As only buz to heav'n with ev'ning wings;

Strike

Strike in the dark, offending but by chance,
Such are the blind-fold blows of ignorance.
They know not beings, and but hate a name,
To them the *Hind* and *Panther* are the fame.

The *Panther* fure the nobleft, next the *Hind*,
And faireft creature of the fpotted kind;
Oh, could her in-born ftains be wafh'd away,
She were too good to be a beaft of Prey!
How can I praife, or blame, and not offend,
Or how divide the frailty from the friend!
Her faults and vertues lye fo mix'd, that fhe
Nor wholly ftands condemn'd, nor wholly free;
Then, like her injur'd *Lyon*, let me fpeak,
He cannot bend her, and he would not break.
Unkind already, and eftrang'd in part,
The *Wolfe* begins to fhare her wandring heart.
Though unpolluted yet with actual ill,
She half commits, who fins but in Her will.

If,

If, as our dreaming *Platonifts* report,

There could be fpirits of a middle fort,

Too black for heav'n, and yet too white for hell,

Who juft dropt half way <u>done</u>, nor lower fell ;

So pois'd, fo gently fhe defcends from high,

It feems a foft difmiffion from the skie.

Her houfe not ancient, whatfoe'er pretence

Her clergy Heraulds make in her defence.

A fecond century not half-way run.

Since the new honours of her blood begun.

A *Lyon* old, obfcene, and furious made

By luft, comprefs'd her mother in a fhade.

Then, by a left-hand marr'age weds the Dame,

Cov'ring adult'ry with a fpecious name:

So fchifm begot ; and facrilege and fhe,

A well-match'd pair, got gracelefs herefie.

God's and Kings rebels have the fame good caufe,

To trample down divine and humane laws :

Both wou'd be call'd Reformers, and their hate,

Alike deftructive both to Church and State:

The

The fruit proclaims the plant; a lawlefs Prince
By luxury reform'd incontinence,
By ruins, charity; by riots, abftinence.
Confeffions, fafts and penance fet afide;
Oh with what eafe we follow fuch a guide!
Where fouls are ftarv'd, and fenfes gratify'd.
Where marr'age pleafures, midnight pray'r fupply,
And mattin bells (a melancholly cry)
Are tun'd to merrier notes, *encreafe* and *multiply.*
Religion fhows a Rofie colour'd face;
Not hatter'd out with drudging works of grace;
A down-hill Reformation rolls apace.
What flefh and blood wou'd croud the narrow gate,
Or, till they wafte their pamper'd paunches, wait;
All wou'd be happy at the cheapeft rate.

Though our lean faith thefe rigid laws has giv'n,
The full fed *Mufulman* goes fat to heav'n;
For his *Arabian* Prophet with delights
Of fenfe, allur'd his eaftern Profelytes.

The

The jolly *Luther*, reading him, began
T'interpret Scriptures by his *Alcoran*;
To grub the thorns beneath our tender feet,
And make the paths of *Paradife* more fweet:
Bethought him of a wife e'er half way gone.
(For 'twas uneafie travailing alone ,)
And in this mafquerade of mirth and love,
Miftook the blifs of heav'n for *Bacchanals* above.
Sure he prefum'd of praife, who came to ftock
Th' etherial paftures with fo fair a flock ;
Burnifh'd, and bat'ning on their food, to fhow
The diligence of carefull herds below.

Onr *Panther*,though like thefe fhe chang'd her head,
Yet, as the miftrefs of a monarch's bed,
Her front erect with majefty fhe bore,
The Crozier weilded, and the Miter wore.
Her upper part of decent difcipline
Shew'd affectation of an ancient line :

And fathers, councils, church and churches head,

Were on her reverend *Phylacteries* read.

But what difgrac'd and difavow'd the reft,

Was *Calvin's* brand, that ftigmatiz'd the beaft.

Thus, like a creature of a double kind,

In her own labyrinth fhe lives confin'd.

To foreign lands no found of Her is come,

Humbly content to be defpis'd at home.

Such is her faith, where good cannot be had,

At leaft fhe leaves the refufe of the bad.

Nice in her choice of ill, though not of beft,

And leaft deform'd, becaufe reform'd the leaft.

In doubtful points betwixt her diff'ring friends,

Where one for fubftance, one for fign contends,

Their contradicting terms fhe ftrives to joyn.

Sign fhall be fubftance, fubftance fhall be fign.

A real prefence all her fons allow,

And yet 'tis flat Idolatry to bow,

Becaufe the God-head's there they know not how.

Her

Her Novices are taught that bread and wine
Are but the vifible and outward fign
Receiv'd by thofe who in communion joyn.
But th' inward grace, or the thing fignify'd,
His blood and body, who to fave us dy'd ;
The faithful this thing fignify'd receive.
What is't thofe faithful then partake or leave ?
For what is fignify'd and underftood,
Is, by her own confeffion, flefh and blood.
Then, by the fame acknowledgement, we know
They take the fign, and take the fubftance too,
The litral fenfe is hard to flefh and blood,
But nonfenfe never can be underftood.

Her wild belief on ev'ry wave is toft,
But fure no Church can better morals boaft.
True to her King her principles are found ;
Oh that her practice were but half fo found !
Stedfaft in various turns of ftate fhe ftood,
And feal'd her vow'd affection with her blood ;

Nor

Nor will I meanly tax her conſtancy,

That int'reſt or obligement made the tye,

(Bound to the fate of murdr'd Monarchy:)

(Before the founding Ax ſo falls the Vine,

Whoſe tender branches round the Poplar twine.)

She choſe her ruin, and reſign'd her life,

In death undaunted as an *Indian* wife :

A rare example: But ſome ſouls we ſee

Grow hard, and ſtiffen with adverſity :

Yet theſe by fortunes favours are undone,

Reſolv'd into a baſer form they run,

And bore the wind, but cannot bear the ſun.

Let this be natures frailty or her fate,

Or * *Iſgrim's* counſel, her new choſen mate ;   * *The Wolfe.*]

Still ſhe's the faireſt of the fallen Crew,

No mother more indulgent but the true.

Fierce to her foes, yet fears her force to try,

Becauſe ſhe wants innate auctority ;

E   For

For how can she conftrain them to obey
Who has her felf caft off the lawful fway ?
Rebellion equals all, and thofe who toil
In common theft, will fhare the common fpoil.
Let her produce the title and the right
Againft her old fuperiours firft to fight ;
If fhe reform by Text, ev'n that's as plain.
For her own Rebels to reform again.
As long as words a diff'rent fenfe will bear;
And each may be his own Interpreter;
Our ai'ry faith will no foundation find:
The word's a weathercock for ev'ry wind:
The *Bear* the *Fox*, the *Wolfe*, by turns prevail,
The moft in pow'r fupplies the prefent gale.
The wretched *Panther* crys aloud for aid.
To church and councils, whom fhe firft betray'd;
No help from Fathers or traditions train,
Thofe ancient guides fhe taught us to difdain.
And by that fcripture which fhe once abus'd.
To Reformation, ftands her felf accus'd.

What

What bills for breach of laws can she prefer,

Expounding which she owns her self may err?

And, after all her winding ways are try'd,

If doubts arise she slips herself aside,

And leaves the private conscience for the guide.

If then that conscience set th' offender free,

It bars her claim to church auctority.

How can she censure, or what crime pretend,

But Scripture may be conftru'd to defend?

Ev'n those whom for rebellion she tranfmits

To civil pow'r, her doctrine firft acquits;

Becaufe no difobedience can enfue,

Where no fubmiffion to a Judge is due.

Each judging for himfelf, by her confent,

Whom thus abfolv'd she fends to punishment.

Suppofe the Magiftrate revenge her caufe,

'Tis only for tranfgreffing humane laws.

How anfw'ring to its end a church is made,

Whofe pow'r is but to counfel and perfwade?

O folid

O folid rock, on which fecure fhe ftands !
Eternal houfe, not built with mortal hands !
O fure defence againft th' infernal gate,
A patent during pleafure of the ftate !

Thus is the *Panther* neither lov'd nor fear'd,
A meer mock Queen of a divided Herd ;
Whom foon by lawful pow'r fhe might controll,
Her felf a part fubmitted to the whole.
Then, as the Moon who firft receives the light
By which fhe makes our nether regions bright,
So might fhe fhine, reflecting from afar
The rays fhe borrow'd from a better Star :
Big with the beams which from her mother flow
And reigning o'er the rifing tides below :
Now, mixing with a falvage croud, fhe goes,
And meanly flatters her invet'rate foes,
Rul'd while fhe rules, and lofing ev'ry hour
Her wretched remnants of precarious pow'r.

One

One evening while the cooler ſhade ſhe ſought,
Revolving many a melancholy thought,
Alone ſhe walk'd, and look'd around in vain,
With ruful viſage for her vaniſh'd train: ·
None of her ſylvan ſubjects made their court ;
Leveés and coucheés paſs'd without reſort.
So hardly can Uſurpers manage well
Thoſe, whom they firſt inſtructed to rebel :
More liberty begets deſire of more,
The hunger ſtill encreaſes with the ſtore.
Without reſpect they bruſh'd along the wood
Each in his clan, and fill'd with loathſome food,
Ask'd no permiſſion to the neighb'ring flood,
The *Panther,* full of inward diſcontent,
Since they wou'd goe, before 'em wiſely went::
Supplying want of pow'r by drinking firſt,
As if ſhe gave 'em leave to quench their thirſt.
Among the reſt, the *Hind,* with fearful face
Beheld from far the common wat'ring place,

Nor

Nor durſt approach ; till with an awful roar
The ſovereign *Lyon* bad her fear no more.
Encourag'd thus ſhe brought her younglings nigh,
Watching the motions of her Patron's eye,
And drank a ſober draught ; the reſt amaz'd
Stood mutely ſtill, and on the ſtranger gaz'd :
Survey'd her part by part, and ſought to find
The ten-horn'd monſter in the harmleſs *Hind*,
Such as the *Wolfe* and *Panther* had deſign'd.
They thought at firſt they dream'd, for 'twas offence
With them, to queſtion certitude of ſenſe,
Their guide in faith ; but nearer when they drew,
And had the faultleſs object full in view,
Lord, how they all admir'd her heav'nly hiew !
Some, who before her fellowſhip diſdain'd,
Scarce, and but ſcarce, from in-born rage reſtrain'd,
Now friſk'd about her, and old kindred feign'd.
Whether for love or int'reſt, ev'ry ſect
Of all the ſalvage nation ſhew'd reſpect:

The

TheVice-roy *Panther* could not awe the herd,
The more the company the lefs they fear'd.
The furly *Wolfe* with fecret envy burft,
Yet cou'd not howl, the *Hind* had feen him firft:
But what he durft not fpeak, the *Panther* durft.

For when the herd fuffis'd, did late repair
To ferney heaths, and to their foreft lare,
She made a mannerly excufe to ftay,
Proff'ring the *Hind* to wait her half the way :
That fince the Skie was clear, an hour of talk
Might help her to beguile the tedious walk.
With much good-will the motion was embrac'd,
To chat awhile on their adventures pafs'd:
Nor had the grateful *Hind* fo foon forgot
Her friend and fellow-fuff'rer in the plot:
Yet wondring how of late fhe grew eftrang'd;
Her forehead cloudy, and her count'nance chang'd,
She thought this hour th' occafion would prefent
To learn her fecret caufe of difcontent,

Which.

Which, well fhe hop'd, might be with eafe redrefs'd,
Confid'ring Her a well-bred civil beaft,
And more a Gentlewoman than the reft.
After fome common talk what rumours ran,
The Lady of the fpotted-muff began.

THE

THE
HIND
AND THE
PANTHER.

The Second Part.

DAME, said the *Panther*, times are mended well
Since late among the *Philistines* you fell ;
The Toils were pitch'd, a spacious tract of ground
With expert Huntsmen was encompass'd round ;
Th' Enclosure narrow'd ; the sagacious pow'r
Of Hounds, and Death drew nearer eve'ry Hour.

'Tis true, the younger *Lyon* fcap'd the fnare,
But all your prieftly Calves lay ftrugling there ;
As facrifices on their Altars laid ;
While you their careful mother wifely fled
Not trufting deftiny to fave your head.
For, what e'er Promifes you have apply'd
To your unfailing Church, the furer fide
Is four fair Leggs in danger to provide.
And what e'er Tales of *Peter's* Chair you tell,
Yet faving Reverence of the Miracle,
The better luck was yours to 'fcape fo well.

As I remember, faid the fober *Hind,*
Thofe Toils were for your own dear felf defign'd,
As well as me ; and, with the felf fame throw,
To catch the Quarry and the Vermin too,
(Forgive the fland'rous Tongues that call'd you fo.)
Howe'er you take it now, the common Cry
Then ran you down for your rank Loyalty;

Befides, in Popery they thought you nurft,

(As evil tongues ame, er fpeak the worft,)

Becaufe fome forms, and ceremonies fome

You kept, and ftood in the main queftion dumb.

Dumb you were born indeed, but thinking long

The *Teft* it feems at laft has loos'd your tongue.

And, to explain what your forefathers meant,

By real prefence in the Sacrament,

(After long fencing pufh'd againft a wall,)

Your *falvo* comes, that he's not there at all :

There chang'd your faith, and what may change may fall.

Who can believe what varies every day,

Nor ever was, nor will be at a ftay ?

Tortures may force the tongue untruths to tell,

And I ne'er own'd my felf infallible,

Reply'd the *Panther* ; grant fuch Prefence were,

Yet in your fenfe I never own'd it there.

A real *vertue* we by faith receive,

And that we in the facrament believe.

Then

Then said the *Hind*, as you the m————ate

Not only *Jesuits* can equivocate ;

For *real*, as you now the Word expound,

From Solid Substance dwindles to a Sound.

Methinks an *Esop*'s fable you repeat,

You know who took the Shadow for the Meat ;

Your Churches substance thus you change at will,

And yet retain your former figure still!

I freely grant you spoke to save your Life,

For then you lay beneath the Buther's Knife:

Long time you fought, redoubl'd Batt'ry bore,

But, after all, against your self you swore;

Your former self, for ev'ry Hour your form

Is chop'd and chang'd, like Winds before a Storm.

Thus Fear and Int'rest will prevail with some,

For all have not the ·Gift of· Martyrdom.

The *Panter* grin'd at this, and thus reply'd ;

That men may err was never yet deny'd.

But,

But, if that common principle be true,
The Cannon, Dame, is level'd full at you.
But, fhunning long difputes, I fain wou'd fee
That wond'rous Wight, infallibility.
Is he from Heav'n this mighty Champion come,
Or lodg'd below in fubterranean *Rome* ?
Firft, feat him fomewhere, and derive his Race,
Or elfe conclude that nothing has no place.

Suppofe (though I difown it) faid the *Hind*,
The certain Manfion were not yet affign'd,
The doubtful refidence no proof can bring
Againft the plain exiftence of the thing.
Becaufe *Philofophers* may difagree,
If Sight b'emiffion or reception be,
Shall it be thence infer'd, I do not fee?
But you require an Anfwer pofitive,
Which yet, when I demand, you dare not give,
For Fallacies in Univerfals live.

E

I then affirm that this unfailing guide
In Pope and gen'ral Councils muft refide ;
Both lawful, both combin'd, what one decrees
By numerous Votes, the other Ratifies :
On this undoubted Senfe the Church relies.
Tis true, fome Doctors in a fcantier fpace,
I mean in each apart contract the Place.
Some, who to greater length extend the Line,
The Churches after acceptation join.
This laft Circumference appears too wide,
The Church diffus'd is by the Council ty'd ;
As members by their Reprefentatives
Oblig'd to Laws which Prince and Senate gives :
Thus fome contract, and fome enlarge the fpace ;
In Pope and Council who denies the place,
Affifted from above with God's unfailing grace ?
Thofe Canons all the needful points contain ;
Their fenfe fo obvious, and their words fo plain,
That no difputes about the doubtful Text
Have, hitherto, the lab'ring world perplex'd :

If any fhou'd in after times appear,

New Councils muft be call'd, to make the meaning clear.

Becaufe in them the pow'r fupreme refides ;.

And all the promifes are to the Guides.

This may be taught with found and fafe Defence :

But mark how fandy is your own pretence,

Who fetting Councils, Pope, and Church afide,

Are ev'ry Man his own prefuming Guide.

The facred Books you fay, are full and plain,

And ev'ry needful Point of Truth contain :

All who can read, Interpreters may be :

Thus though your feveral Churches difagree,

Yet ev'ry Saint has to himfelf alone

The Secret of this Philofophick Stone.

Thefe Principles you jarring Sects unite,

When diff'ring Doctors and Difciples Fight.

Though *Luther, Zuinglius, Calvin,* holy Chiefs

Have made a Battel Royal of Beliefs ;

Or like wild Horfes fev'ral ways have whirl'd.

The tortur'd Text about the Chriftian World ;.

Each

Each *Jebu* lashing on with furious force,
That *Turk* or *Jew* cou'd not have us'd it worse.
No matter what dissention leaders make
Where ev'ry private man may have a stake
Rul'd by the Scripture and his own advice
Each has a blind-by-path to Paradise ;
Where driving in a Circle slow or fast,
Oppoſing Sects are ſure to meet at laſt.
A wondrous charity you have in Store
For all reform'd to paſs the narrow Door :
So much, that *Mahomet* had ſcarcely more.
For he, kind Prophet, was for damning none,
But *Chriſt* and *Moyſes* were to ſave their own :
Himſelf was to ſecure his choſen race,
Though reaſon good for *Turks* to take the place,
And he allow'd to be the better Man
In virtue of his holier *Alcoran.*

True, ſaid the *Panther,* I ſhall ne'er deny
My Breth'ren may be ſav'd as well as I :

Though

Though *Huguenots* contemn our ordination,
Succeffion, minifterial vocation;
And *Luther,* more miftaking what he read,
Misjoins the facred Body with the Bread;
Yet, *Lady,* ftill remember I maintain,
The Word in needfull points is only plain.

Needlefs or needful I not now contend,
For ftill you have a loop-hole for a friend,
(Rejoyn'd the Matron) but the rule you lay
Has led whole flocks, and leads them ftill aftray
In weighty points, and full damnation's way.
For did not *Arius* firft, *Socinus* now,
The Son's eternal god-head difavow,
And did not thefe by Gofpel Texts alone
Condemn our doctrine, and maintain their own?
Have not all hereticks the fame pretence
To plead the Scriptures in their own defence?
How did the *Nicene* council then decide
That ftrong debate, was it by Scripture try'd?

No fure to thofe the Rebel would not yield,
Squadrons of Texts he marfhal'd in the field;
That was but civil war, an equal fet,
Where Piles with piles, and Eagles Eagles met.
With Texts point-blank and plain he fac'd the Foe:
And did not *Sathan* tempt our Saviour fo?
The good old Bifhops took a fimpler way,
Each ask'd but what he heard his Father fay,
Or how he was inftructed in his youth,
And by traditions force upheld the truth.

The *Panther* fmil'd at this, and when, faid fhe,
Were thofe firft Councils difallow'd by me?
Or where did I at fure tradition ftrike,
Provided ftill it were Apoftolick?

Friend, faid the *Hind*, you quit your former ground,
Where all your Faith you did on Scripture found,
Now, 'tis tradition join'd with holy writ,
But thus your memory betrays your wit.

No,

No, faid. the *Panther*, for in that I view,
When your tradition's forg'd, and when 'tis true.
I fet 'em by the rule, and as they fquare,
Or deviate from undoubted doctrine there,
This Oral fiction, that old Faith declare.

(*Hind.*) The Council fteer'd it feems a diff'rent courfe,
They try'd the Scripture by tradition's force;
But you tradition by the Scripture try;
Purfu'd, by Sects, from this to that you fly,
Nor dare on one foundation to rely.
The word is then depos'd, and in this view,
You rule the Scripture, not the Scripture you.
Thus faid the *Dame*, and fmiling, thus purfu'd,
I fee tradition then is difallow'd,
When not evinc'd by Scripture to be true,
And Scripture, as interpreted by you.
But here you tread upon unfaithfull ground;
Unlefs you cou'd infallibly expound.

G 2 Which

Which you reject as odious Popery,

And throw that doctrine back with scorn on me,

Suppose we on things traditive divide,

And both appeal to Scripture to decide;

By various texts we both uphold our claim,

Nay, often ground our titles on the same :

After long labour loft, and times expence,

Both grant the words, and quarrel for the fenfe.

Thus all difputes for ever mult depend;

For no dumb rule can controverfies end.

Thus when you faid tradition mult be try'd

By Sacred Writ, whofe fenfe your felves decide,

You faid no more, but that your felves mult be

The judges of the Scripture fenfe, not we.

Againft our church tradition you declare

And yet your Clerks wou'd fit in *Moyfes* chair :

At leaft 'tis prov'd againft your argument,

The rule is far from plain, where all diffent.

If

If not by Scriptures how can we be fure
(Reply'd the *Panther*) what tradition's pure?
For you may palm upon us new for old,
All, as they fay, that glitters is not gold.

How but by following her, reply'd the Dame,
To whom deriv'd from fire to fon they came;
Where ev'ry age do's on another move,
And trufts no farther than the next above;
Where all the rounds like *Jacob's* ladder rife,
The loweft hid in earth, the topmoft in the skyes.

    Sternly the falvage did her anfwer mark,
Her glowing eye-balls glitt'ring in the dark,
And faid but this, fince lucre was your trade,
Succeeding times fuch dreadfull gaps have made
'Tis dangerous climbing: to your fons and you
I leave the ladder, and its omen too.

The

(*Hind.*) The *Panther's* breath was ever fam'd for fweet,
But from the *Wolf* fuch wifhes oft I meet:
You learn'd this language from the blatant beaft,
Or rather did not fpeak, but were poffefs'd.
As for your anfwer 'tis but barely urg'd;
You muft evince tradition to be forg'd;
Produce plain proofs; unblemifh'd author's ufe
As ancient as thofe ages they accufe;
Till when 'tis not fufficient to defame:
An old poffeffion ftands, till Elder quitts the claim.
Then for our int'reft which is nam'd alone
To load with envy, we retort your own.
For when traditions in your faces fly,
Refolving not to yield, you muft decry:
As when the caufe goes hard, the guilty man
Excepts, and thins his jury all he can;
So when you ftand of other aid bereft,
You to the twelve Apoftles would be left.

Your

Your friend the *Wolfe* did with more craft provide

To fet thofe toys traditions quite afide:

And *Fathers* too, unlefs when reafon fpent

He cites 'em but fometimes for ornament.

But, Madam *Panther*, you, though more fincere,

Are not fo wife as your Adulterer:

The private fpirit is a better blind

Than all the dodging tricks your authours find.

For they, who left the Scripture to the crowd,

Each for his own peculiar judge allow'd;

The way to pleafe 'em was to make 'em proud.

Thus, with full fails, they ran upon the fhelf;

Who cou'd fufpect a couzenage from himfelf?

On his own reafon fafer 'tis to ftand,

Than be deceiv'd and damn'd at fecond hand.

But you who *Fathers* and traditions take,

And garble fome, and fome you quite forfake,

Pretending church auctority to fix,

And yet fome grains of private fpirit mix.

Are

Are like a *Mule* made up of diff'ring feed,

And that's the reafon why you never breed;

At leaft not propagate your kind abroad,

For home diffenters are by ftatutes aw'd:

And yet they grow upon you ev'ry day,

While you (to fpeak the beft) are at a ftay,

For fects that are extremes, abhor a middle way.

Like tricks of ftate, to ftop a raging flood,

Or mollify a mad-brain'd Senate's mood:

Of all expedients never one was good.

Well may they argue, (nor can you deny)

If we muft fix on church auctority,

Beft on the beft, the fountain, not the flood,

That muft be better ftill, if this be good.

Shall fhe command, who has her felf rebell'd?

Is *Antichrift* by *Antichrift* expell'd?

Did we a lawfull tyranny difplace,

To fet aloft a baftard of the race ?

Why all thefe wars to win the Book, if we

Muft not interpret for our felves, but fhe?

Either be wholly flaves or wholly free.

For *purging* fires traditions muft not fight;

But they muft prove Epifcopacy's right:

Thus thofe led horfes are from fervice freed;

You never mount 'em but in time of need.

Like mercenary's, hir'd for home defence,

They will not ferve againft their native Prince.

Againft domeftick foes of *Hierarchy*

Thefe are drawn forth, to make fanaticks fly;

But, when they fee their countrey-men at hand,

Marching againft 'em under church-command,

Streight they forfake their colours, and disband.

Thus fhe, nor cou'd the *Panther* well enlarge

With weak defence againft fo ftrong a charge;

But faid, for what did *Chrift* his Word provide,

If ftill his church muft want a living guide?

And if all faving doctrines are not there,

Or facred Pen-men cou'd not make 'em clear,

H

From

From after-ages we fhould hope in vain
For truths, which men infpir'd, cou'd not explain.

Before the Word was written, faid the *Hind:*
Our Saviour preach'd his Faith to humane kind;
From his Apoftles the firft age receiv'd
Eternal truth, and what they taught, believ'd.
Thus by tradition faith was planted firft,
Succeeding flocks fucceeding Paftours nurs'd.
This was the way our wife Redeemer chofe,
(Who fure could all things for the beft difpofe,)
To fence his fold from their encroaching foes.
He cou'd have writ himfelf, but well forefaw
Th' event would be like that of *Moyfes* law;
Some difference wou'd arife, fome doubts remain,
Like thofe, which yet the jarring *Jews* maintain.
No written laws can be fo plain, fo pure,
But wit may glofs, and malice may obfcure,
Not thofe indited by his firft command,
A Prophet grav'd the text, an Angel held his hand.

Thus

Thus faith was e'er the written word appear'd,
And men believ'd, not what they read, but heard.
But fince the Apoftles cou'd not be confin'd,
To thefe, or thofe, but feverally defign'd
Their large commiffion round the world to blow ;
To fpread their faith they fpread their labours too.
Yet ftill their abfent flock their pains did fhare,
They hearken'd ftill, for love produces care.
And as miftakes arofe, or difcords fell,
Or bold feducers taught 'em to rebell,
As charity grew cold, or faction hot,
Or long neglect their leffons had forgot,
For all their wants they wifely did provide,
And preaching by Epiftles was fupply'd :
So great Phyficians cannot all attend,
But fome they vifit, and to fome they fend.
Yet all thofe letters were not writ to all ;
Nor firft intended, but occafional.
Their abfent fermons ; nor if they contain
All needfull doctrines, are thofe doctrines plain.

Clearnefs

Clearnefs by frequent preaching muft be wrought,
They writ but feldom, but they daily taught.
And what one Saint has faid of holy *Paul*,
He darkly writ, is true apply'd to all.
For this obfcurity cou'd heav'n provide
More prudently than by a living guide,
As doubts arofe, the difference to decide?
A guide was therefore needfull, therefore made;
And, if appointed, fure to be obey'd.
Thus, with due rev'rence to th' Apoftles writ,
By which my fons are taught, to which, fubmit;
I think, thofe truths their facred works contain,
The church alone can certainly explain;
That following ages, leaning on the paft,
May reft upon the Primitive at laft.
Nor wou'd I thence the word no rule infer,
But none without the church interpreter.
Becaufe, as I have urg'd before, 'tis mute,
And is it felf the fubject of difpute.

But

But what th'Apostles their successours taught,
They to the next, from them to us is brought,
Th'undoubted sense which is in scripture sought.

From hence the church is arm'd, when errours rise,
To stop their entrance, and prevent surprise;
And safe entrench'd within, her foes without defies.

By these all festring sores her counsels heal,
Which time or has discloas'd, or shall reveal,
For discord cannot end without a last appeal.

Nor can a council national decide
But with subordination to her Guide:
(I wish the cause were on that issue try'd.)

Much less the scripture; for suppose debate
Betwixt pretenders to a fair estate,
Bequeath'd by some Legator's last intent;
(Such is our dying Saviour's Testament:)
The will is prov'd, is open'd, and is read;
The doubtfull heirs their diff'ring titles plead:
All vouch the words their int'rest to maintain,
And each pretends by those his cause is plain.

Shall

Shall then the teftament award the right?

No, that's the *Hungary* for which they fight;

The field of battel, fubject of debate;

The thing contended for, the fair eftate.

The fenfe is intricate, 'tis onely clear

What vowels and what confonants are there.

Therefore 'tis plain, its meaning muft be try'd

Before fome judge appointed to decide.

Suppofe, (the fair Apoftate faid,) I grant,

The faithfull flock fome living guide fhould want,

Your arguments an endlefs chafe perfue:

Produce this vaunted Leader to our view,

This mighty *Moyfes* of the chofen crew.

The Dame, who faw her fainting foe retir'd;

With force renew'd, to victory afpir'd;

(And looking upward to her kindred sky,

As once our Saviour own'd his Deity,

Pronounc'd his words—*fhe whom ye feek am I.*)

                                                    Nor

Nor lefs amaz'd this voice the *Panther* heard,
Than were thofe *Jews* to hear a god declar'd.
Then thus the matron modeftly renew'd;
Let all your prophets and their fects be view'd,
And fee to which of 'em your felves think fit
The conduct of your confcience to fubmit :
Each Profelyte wou'd vote his Doctor beft,
With abfolute exclufion to the reft :
Thus wou'd your *Polifh* Diet difagree,
And end as it began in Anarchy :
Your felf the faireft for election ftand,
Becaufe you feem crown-gen'ral of the land ;
But foon againft your fuperftitious lawn
Some Presbyterian Sabre wou'd be drawn :
In your eftablifh'd laws of fov'raignty
The reft fome fundamental flaw wou'd fee,
And call Rebellion gofpel-liberty.
To church-decrees your articles require
Submiffion modify'd if not entire ;

Homage

Homage deny'd, to censures you proceed;
But when *Curtana* will not doe the deed,
You lay that pointlefs clergy-weapon by,
And to the laws, your fword of justice fly.
Now this your fects the more unkindly take
(Thofe prying varlets hit the blots you make)
Becaufe fome ancient friends of yours declare,
Your onely rule of faith the Scriptures are,
Interpreted by men of judgment found,
Which ev'ry fect will for themfelves expound:
Nor think lefs rev'rence to their doctours due
For found interpretation, than to you:
If then, by able heads, are underftood
Your brother prophets, who reform'd abroad,
Thofe able heads expound a wifer way,
That their own fheep their fhepherd fhou'd obey.
But if you mean your felves are onely found,
That doctrine turns the reformation round,
And all the reft are falfe reformers found.

Becaufe

Becaufe in fundry Points you ftand-alone,

Not in Communion join'd with any one ;

And therefore muft be all the Church, or none.

Then, till you have agreed whofe judge is beft,

Againft this forc'd fubmiffion they proteft :

While *found* and *found* a diff'rent fenfe explains

Both play at-hard-head till they break their brains :

And from their Chairs each others force defy,

While unregarded thunders vainly fly.

I pafs the reft, becaufe your Church alone

Of all Ufurpers beft cou'd fill the Throne.

But neither you, nor any Sect befide

For this high Office can be qualify'd,

With neceffary Gifts requir'd in fuch a Guide.

For that which muft direct the whole, muft be

Bound in one Bond of Faith and Unity :

But all your fev'ral Churches difagree.

The *Confubftantiating* Church and Prieft

Refufe Communion to the *Calvinift* ;

The *French* reform'd, from Preaching you reftrain,

Becaufe you judge their Ordination vain;

And fo they judge of yours, but Donors muft ordain.

In fhort in Doctrine, or in Difcipline

Not one reform'd, can with another join:

But all from each, as from Damnation fly;

No Union they pretend, but in *Non-Popery*.

Nor fhould their Members in a Synod meet,

Cou'd any Church prefume to mount the Seat

Above the reft, their difcords to decide;

None wou'd obey, but each wou'd be the Guide:

And face to face Diffentions wou'd encreafe;

For only diftance now preferves the Peace.

All in their Turns accufers, and accus'd:

Babel was never half fo much confus'd.

What one can plead, the reft can plead as well;

For amongft equals lies no laft appeal,

And all confefs themfelves are fallible.

Now fince you grant fome neceffary Guide,

All who can err are juftly laid afide:

Becaufe

Becaufe a truft fo facred to confer

Shows want of fuch a fure Interpreter :

And how can he be needful who can err ?

Then granting that unerring guide we want,

That fuch there is you ftand oblig'd to grant :

Our Saviour elfe were wanting to fupply

Our needs, and obviate that Neceffity.

It then remains that Church can only be

The Guide, which owns unfailing certainty ;

Or elfe you flip your hold, and change your fide,

Relapfing from a neceffary Guide.

But this annex'd Condition of the Crown,

Immunity from Errours, you difown,

Here then you fhrink, and lay your weak pretenfions down.

For petty Royalties you raife debate ;

But this unfailing Univerfal State

You fhun : nor dare fucceed to fuch a glorious weight.

And for that caufe thofe Promifes deteft

With which our Saviour did his Church inveft :

But ſtrive t'evade, and fear to find 'em true,
As conſcious they were never meant to you :
All which the mother church aſſerts her own,
And with unrivall'd claim aſcends the throne.
So when of old th'Almighty father ſate
In Council,to redeem our ruin'd ſtate, ·
Millions of millions at a diſtance round,
Silent the ſacred Conſiſtory crown'd,
To hear what mercy mixt with Juſtice cou'd propound.
All prompt with eager pity, to fulfill
The full extent of their Creatour's will :
But when the ſtern conditions were declar'd,
A mournful whiſper through the hoſt was heard,
And the whole hierarchy, with heads hung down,
Submiſſively declin'd the pondrous proffer'd crown.
Then, not till then, th'eternal Son from high
Roſe in the ſtrength of all the Deity ;
Stood forth t'accept the terms, and underwent
A weight which all the frame of heav'n had bent,
Nor he Himſelf cou'd bear, but as omnipotent.

Now, to remove the leaſt remaining doubt,
That ev'n the blear-ey'd ſects may find her out,
Behold what heav'nly rays adorn her brows,
What from his Wardrobe her belov'd allows
To deck the wedding-day of his unſpotted ſpouſe:
Behold what marks of Majeſty ſhe brings ;
Richer than antient heirs of Eaſtern kings :
Her right hand holds the ſceptre and the keys,
To ſhew whom ſhe commands, and who obeys :
With theſe to bind, or ſet the ſinner free,
With that t' aſſert ſpiritual Royalty.

    One in herſelf not rent by Schiſm, but found,
Entire, one ſolid ſhining Diamond,

Marks of the Catholick Church from the Nicene. Creed.

Not Sparkles ſhatter'd into Sects like you;
One is the Church, and muſt be to be true :
One central principle of unity.
    As undivided, ſo from errours free,
As one in faith, ſo one in ſanctity.

Thus

·Thus she, and none but she, th' insulting Rage

Of Hereticks oppos'd from Age to Age:

Still when the Giant-brood invades her Throne

She stoops from Heav'n, and meets 'em half way down,

And with paternal Thunder vindicates her Crown.

But like *Egyptian* Sorcerers you stand,

And vainly lift aloft yonr Magick Wand,

To sweep away the Swarms of Vermin from the Land:

You cou'd like them, with like infernal Force

Produce the Plague, but not arrest the Course.

But when the Boils and Botches, with disgrace

And publick Scandal sat upon the Face,

Themselves attack'd, the *Magi* strove no more,

They saw God's Finger, and their Fate deplore;

Themselves they cou'd not Cure of the dishonest sore.

Thus one, thus pure, behold her largely spread

Like the fair Ocean from her Mother-Bed;

From East to West triumphantly she rides,

All Shoars are water'd by her wealthy Tides.

The Gospel-found diffus'd from Pole to Pole,
Where winds can carry, and where waves can roll.
The self same doctrin of the Sacred Page
Convey'd to ev'ry clime in ev'ry age.

Here let my sorrow give my satyr place,
To raise new blushes on my *British* race ;
Our sayling Ships like common shoars we use,
And through our diftant Colonies diffufe
The draughts of Dungeons, and the stench of stews.
Whom, when their home-bred honesty is loft,
We disembogue on some far *Indian* coast :
Thieves, Pandars, Palliards, sins of ev'ry sort,
Those are the manufactures we export ;
And these the *Misfioners* our zeal has made :
For, with my Countrey's pardon be it said,
Religion is the least of all our trade.

Yet

Yet some improve their traffick more than we,
For they on gain, their only God, rely :
And set a publick price on piety.
Induftrious of the needle and the chart
They run full fail to their *Japponian* Mart :
Prevention fear, and prodigal of fame
Sell all of Chriftian to the very name ;
Nor leave enough of that,to hide their naked fhame.

Thus, of three marks which in the Creed we view,
Not one of all can be apply'd to you :
Much lefs the fourth ; in vain alas you feek
Th' ambitious title of. Apoftolick :
God-like defcent ! 'tis well your bloud can be
Prov'd noble, in the third or fourth degree :
For all of ancient that you had before,
(I mean what is not borrow'd from our ftore)
Was Errour fulminated o'er and o'er.

Old

Old Herefies condemn'd in ages paft,
By care and time recover'd from the blaft.'

'Tis faid with eafe, but never can be prov'd,
The church her old foundations has remov'd,
And built new doctrines on unftable fands :
Judge that ye winds and rains; you prov'd her,yet fhe ftands
Thofe ancient doctrines charg'd on her for new,
Shew when, and how, and from what hands they grew.
We claim no pow'r when Herefies grow bold
To coin new faith, but ftill declare the old.
How elfe cou'd that obfcene difeafe be purg'd
When controverted texts are vainly urg'd?
To prove tradition new, there's fomewhat more
Requir'd, than faying, 'twas not us'd before.
Thofe monumental arms are never ftirr'd
Till Schifm or Herefie call down *Goliah's* fword.

Thus, what you call corruptions, are in truth,
The firft plantations of the gofpel's youth,

       K   Old

Old ſtandard faith : but caſt your eyes again
And view thoſe errours which new ſects maintain,
Or which of old diſturb'd the churches peaceful reign,

And we can point each period of the time,
When they began, and who begot the crime;
Can calculate how long th'eclipſe endur'd,
Who interpos'd, what digits were obſcur'd:
Of all which are already paſs'd away,
We know the riſe, the progreſs and decay.

Deſpair at our foundations then to ſtrike
Till you can prove your faith Apoſtolick;
A limpid ſtream drawn from the native ſource;
Succeſſion lawfull in a lineal courſe.
Prove any church oppos'd to this our head,
So one, ſo pure, ſo unconfin'dly ſpread,
Under one chief of the ſpiritual ſtate,
The members all combin'd, and all ſubordinate.
Shew ſuch a ſeamleſs coat, from ſchiſm ſo free,
In no communion join'd with hereſie:

If

If fuch a one you find, let truth prevail:
Till when your weights will in the balance fail:
A church unprincipl'd kicks up the fcale.

But if you cannot think, (nor fure you can
Suppofe in God what were unjuft in man,)
That he, the fountain of eternal grace,
Should fuffer falfhood for fo long a fpace
To banifh truth, and to ufurp her place :
That feav'n fucceffive ages fhould be loft
And preach damnation at their proper coft;
That all your erring anceftours fhould dye,
Drown'd in th' Abyfs of deep Idolatry;
If piety forbid fuch thoughts to rife,
Awake and open your unwilling eyes:
God has left nothing for each age undone,
From this to that wherein he fent his Son:
Then think but well of him, and half your work is done.

See how his church adorn'd with ev'ry grace
With open arms, a kind forgiving face,
Stands ready to prevent her long loſt ſons embrace.
Not more did *Joſeph* o'er his brethren weep,
Nor leſs himſelf cou'd from diſcovery keep,
When in the croud of ſuppliants they were ſeen,
And in their crew his beſt beloved *Benjamin.*
That pious *Joſeph* in the church behold,
To feed your famine, and refuſe your gold ;
The *Joſeph* you exil'd, the *Joſeph* whom you ſold.

The renun-
ciation of
the Bene-
dictines to
the Abby
Lands.

Thus, while with heav'nly charity ſhe ſpoke,
A ſtreaming blaze the ſilent ſhadows broke ;
Shot from the skyes : a chearfull azure light ;
The birds obſcene to foreſts wing'd their flight,
And gaping graves receiv'd the wandring guilty ſpright.

Such were the pleaſing triumphs of the sky
For *James* his late nocturnal victory ;

The

The pledge of his Almighty patron's love,

The fire-works which his angel made above.

I faw my felf the lambent eafie. light   *Pe'ta lo-*
quitur.

Guild the brown horrour and difpell the night;

The meffenger with fpeed the tidings bore;

News which three lab'ring nations did reftore,

But heav'ns own *Nuntius* was arriv'd before.

By this, the *Hind* had reach'd her lonely cell;

And vapours rofe, and dews unwholefome fell.

When fhe, by frequent obfervation wife,

As one who long on heav'n had fix'd her eyes,

Difcern'd a change of weather in the skyes.

The Weftern borders were with crimfon fpread;

The moon defcending look'd all flaming red;

She thought good manners bound her to invite

The ftranger Dame to be her gueft that night.

'Tis true, courfe dyet and a fhort repaft,

(She faid) were weak inducements to the taft

Of one fo nicely bred, and fo unus'd to faft.

                                         But

But what plain fare her cottage cou'd afford,
A hearty welcome at a homely board
Was freely hers; and to supply the reft,
An honeft meaning, and an open breaft.
Laft, with content of mind, the poor man's Wealth;
A grace-cup to their common Patron's health.
This fhe defir'd her to accept and ftay,
For fear fhe might be wilder'd in her way,
Becaufe fhe wanted an unerring guide,
And then the dew-drops on her filken hide
Her tender conftitution did declare,
Too Lady-like a long fatigue to bear,
And rough inclemencies of raw nocturnal air.

But moft fhe fear'd that travelling fo late,
Some evil minded beafts might lye in wait;
And without witnefs wreak their hidden hate.

The *Panther*, though fhe lent a lift'ning ear,
Had more of *Lyon* in her than to fear:

Yet wisely weighing, since she had to deal

With many foes, their numbers might prevail,

Return'd her all the thanks she cou'd afford;

And took her friendly hostess at her word,

Who ent'ring first her lowly roof, (a shed

With hoary mofs and winding Ivy spread,

Honeft enough to hide an humble Hermit's head,)

Thus gracioufly befpoke her welcome gueft :

So might thefe walls, with your fair prefence bleft

Become your dwelling-place of everlafting reft;

Not for a night, or quick revolving year,

Welcome an owner, not a fojourner.

This peaceful Seat my poverty fecures,

War feldom enters but where wealth allures;

Nor yet difpife it, for this poor aboad

Has oft receiv'd, and yet receives a god;

A god victorious of the ftygian race

Here laid his facred limbs, and fanctified the place.

This

This mean retreat did mighty *Pan* contain;
Be emulous of him, and pomp difdain,
And dare not to debafe your foul to gain.

The filent ftranger ftood amaz'd to fee
Contempt of wealth, and wilfull poverty:
And, though ill habits are not foon controll'd,
A while fufpended her defire of gold.
But civily drew in her fharpn'd paws,
Not violating hofpitable laws,
And pacify'd her tail, and lick'd her frothy jaws.

The *Hind* did firft her country Cates provide;
Then couch'd her felf fecurely by her fide.

THE

THE
HIND
AND THE
PANTHER.

The Third Part.

MUCH malice mingl'd with a little wit
Perhaps may cenfure this myfterious writ:
Becaufe the Mufe has peopl'd *Caledon*
With *Panthers*, *Bears* and *Wolves*, and Beafts unknown, }
As if we were not ftock'd with monfters of our own. }

L   Let

Let *Æsop* anfwer, who has fet to view,

Such kinds as *Greece* and *Phrygia* never knew ;

And mother *Hubbard* in her homely drefs

Has fharply blam'd a *Britifh Lionefs*

That *Queen*, whofe foot the factious rabble kee

Expos'd obfcenely naked and a-flee

Led by thofe great examples, may not I

The wanted organs of their words fupply ?

If men tranfact like brutes 'tis equal then

For brutes to claim the privilege of men.

  Others our *Hind* of folly will endite,

To entertain a dang'rous gueft by night.

Let thofe remember that fhe cannot dye

Till rolling time is loft in round eternity ;

Nor need fhe fear the *Panther*, though untam'd,

Becaufe the *Lyon's* peace was now proclaim'd ;

The wary falvage would not give offence,

To forfeit the protection of her *Prince* ;

                                          But

But watch'd the time her vengeance to compleat,
When all her furry fons in frequent Senate met.
Mean while fhe quench'd her fury at the floud,
And with a Lenten fallad cool'd her bloud.
Their commons, though but courfe, were nothing fcant,
Nor did their minds an equal banquet want.

For now the *Hind*, whofe noble nature ftrove
T'exprefs her plain fimplicity of love,
Did all the honours of her houfe fo well,
No fharp debates difturb'd the friendly meal.
She turn'd the talk, avoiding that extreme,
To common dangers paft, a fadly pleafing theam;
Remembring ev'ry ftorm which tofs'd the ftate,
When both were objects of the publick hate,
And drop'd a tear betwixt for her own childrens fate.

Nor fail'd fhe then a full review to make
Of what the *Panther* fuffer'd for her fake.

Her loft efteem, her truth, her loyal care,
Her faith unfhaken to an exil'd Heir,
Her ftrength t'endure, her courage to defy ;
Her choice of honourable infamy.
On thefe prolixly thankfull, fhe enlarg'd,
Then with acknowledgments herfelf fhe charg'd :
For friendfhip of it felf, an holy tye,
Is made more facred by adverfity.
Now fhould they part, malicious tongues wou'd fay,
They met like chance companions on the way,
Whom mutual fear of robbers had poffefs'd ;
While danger lafted, kindnefs was profefs'd ;
But that once o'er, the fhort-liv'd union ends :
The road divides, and there divide the friends.

The *Panther* nodded when her fpeech was done,
And thank'd her coldly in a hollow tone.
But faid her gratitude had gone too far
For common offices of Chriftian care.

If to the lawfull Heir fhe had been true,
She paid but *Cæfar* what was *Cæfar*'s due.
I might, fhe added, with like praife defcribe
Your fuff'ring fons, and fo return your bribe;
But incenfe from my hands is poorly priz'd,
For gifts are fcorn'd where givers are defpis'd.
I ferv'd a turn, and then was caft away;
You, like the gawdy fly, your wings difplay,
And fip the fweets, and bask in your Great *Patron*'s day.

This heard, the *Matron* was not flow to find
What fort of malady had feiz'd her mind;
Difdain, with gnawing envy, fell defpight,
And canker'd malice ftood in open fight.
Ambition, int'reft, pride without controul,
And jealoufie, the jaundice of the foul;
Revenge, the bloudy minifter of ill,
With all the lean tormenters of the will.
'Twas eafie now to guefs from whence arofe
Her new made union with her ancient foes.

Her

Her forc'd civilities, her faint embrace,
Affected kindnefs with an alter'd face:
Yet durft fhe not too deeply probe the wound,
As hoping ftill the nobler parts were found;
But ftrove with Anodynes t'affwage the fmart,
And mildly thus her med'cine did impart.

Complaints of Lovers help to eafe their pain,
It fhows a Reft of kindnefs to complain;
A friendfhip loth to quit its former hold,
And confcious merit may be juftly bold:
But much more juft your jealoufie would fhow,
If others good were injury to you:
Witnefs ye heav'ns how I rejoice to fee
Rewarded worth, and rifing loyalty.
Your Warrier Offspring that upheld the crown,
The fcarlet honours of your peacefull gown;
Are the moft pleafing objects I can find,
Charms to my fight, and cordials to my mind.

When vertue fpooms before a profperous gale.
My heaving wifhes help to fill the fail;
And if my pray'rs for all the brave were heard,
Cæfar fhould ftill have fuch, and fuch fhould ftill reward.

The labour'd earth your pains have fow'd and till'd:
'Tis juft you reap the product of the field.
Yours be the harveft, 'tis the beggars gain
To glean the fallings of the loaded wain.
Such fcatter'd ears as are not worth your care,
Your charity for alms may fafely fpare,
And alms are but the vehicles of pray'r.
My daily bread is litt'rally implor'd,
I have no barns nor granaries to hoard;
If *Cæfar* to his own his hand extends,
Say which of yours his charity offends:
You know he largely gives, to more than are his friends.
Are you defrauded when he feeds the poor?
Our mite decreafes nothing of your ftore;

I am

I am but few, and by your fare you fee
My crying fins are not of luxury.
Some jufter motive fure your mind withdraws, ⎫
And makes you break our friendfhips holy laws, ⎬
For barefac'd envy is too bafe a caufe.   ⎭

   Show more occafion for your difcontent,
Your love, the *Wolf*, wou'd help you to invent;
Some *German* quarrel, or, as times go now,
Some *French*, where force is uppermoft, will doe.
When at the fountains head, as merit ought
To claim the place, you take a fwilling draught,
How eafie 'tis an envious eye to throw,
And tax the fheep for troubling ftreams below;
Or call her, (when no farther caufe you find,)
An enemy profefs'd of all your kind.
But then, perhaps, the wicked World wou'd think,
The *Wolf* defign'd to eat as well as drink.

This

This laſt alluſion gaul'd the *Panther* more,
Becauſe indeed it rubb'd upon the ſore.
Yet ſeem'd ſhe not to winch, though ſhrewdly pain'd:
But thus her Paſſive charaċter maintain'd.

I never grudg'd, whate'er my foes report,
Your flaunting fortune in the *Lyon's* court.
You have your day, or you are much bely'd,
But I am always on the ſuff'ring ſide:
You know my doċtrine, and I need not ſay
I will not, but I cannot diſobey.
On this firm principle I ever ſtood:
He of my ſons who fails to make it good,
By one rebellious aċt renounċs to my bloud.

Ah, ſaid the *Hind*, how many ſons have you
Who call you mother, whom you never knew!
But moſt of them who that relation plead
Are ſuch ungratious youths as wiſh you dead.

They

They gape at rich revenues which you hold,
And fain would nible at your grandame gold;
Enquire into your years, and laugh to find
Your crazy temper shews you much declin'd.
Were you not dim, and doted, you might see
A pack of cheats that claim a pedigree,
No more of kin to you, than you to me.
Do you not know, that for a little coin,
Heralds can foist a name into the line;
They ask you blessing but for what you have,
But once possess'd of what with care you save,
The wanton boyes wou'd pifs upon your grave.

Your fons of Latitude that court your grace,
Though most resembling you in form and face,
Are far the worst of your pretended race.
And, but I blush your honesty to blot:
Pray god you prove 'em lawfully begot :
For, in some *Popish* libells I have read,
The *Wolf* has been too busie in your bed.

At

At leaſt their hinder parts, the belly-piece,
The paunch, and all that *Scorpio* claims are his.
Their malice too a fore fuſpicion brings ;
For though they dare not bark, they ſnarl at kings :
Nor blame 'em for intruding in your line,
Fat Biſhopricks are ſtill of right divine.

Think you your new *French* Profelytes are come
To ſtarve abroad, becauſe they ſtarv'd at home ?
Your benefices twinckl'd from afar,
They found the new, *Meſſiah* by the ſtar :
Thoſe *Swiſſes* fight on any ſide for pay,
And 'tis the living that conforms, not they.
Mark with what management their tribes divide,
Some ſtick to you, and ſome to t'other ſide,
That many churches may for many mouths provide.
More vacant pulpits wou'd more converts make,
All wou'd have Latitude enough to take ;

The reft unbenefic'd, your fects maintain:
For ordinations without cures are vain,
And chamber practice is a filent gain.
Your fons of breadth at home, are much like thefe,,
Their foft and yielding metals run with eafe;
They melt, and take the figure of the mould :
But harden, and preferve it beft in gold.

Your *Delphick* Sword, the *Panther* then reply'd,
Is double edg'd, and cuts on either fide.
Some fons of mine who bear upon their fhield,
Three fteeples Argent in a fable field,
Have fharply tax'd your converts; who unfed
Have follow'd you for miracles of bread;
Such who themfelves of no religion are,
Allur'd with gain, for any will declare:
Bare lyes with bold affertions they can face,
But dint of argument is out of place.
The grim Logician puts 'em in a fright,
'Tis eafier far to flourifh than to fight.

Thus

Thus our eighth Henry's marriage they defame;
. They fay the fchifm of beds began the game,
Divorcing from the *Church* to wed the Dame.

Though largely prov'd, and by himfelf profefs'd
That confcience, confcience wou'd not let him reft :
I mean, not till poffefs'd of her he lov'd,
And old, uncharming *Catherine* was remov'd.
For fundry years before did he complain,
And told his ghoftly Confeffour his pain.
With the fame impudence, without a ground,
They fay, that look the reformation round,
No *Treatife of Humility* is found.
But if none were, the Gofpel does not want,
Our *Saviour* preach'd it, and I hope you grant,
The Sermon in the mount was *Proteftant :*

No doubt, reply'd the *Hind,* as fure as all
The writings of Saint *Peter* and Saint *Paul.*
On that decifion let it ftand or fall.

Now.

Now for my converts, who you say unfed
Have follow'd me for miracles of bread,
Judge not by hear-say, but obferve at leaft,
If fince their change, their loaves have been increaft;
The *Lyon* buyes no Converts, if he did,
Beafts wou'd be fold as faft as he cou'd bid.
Tax thofe of int'reft who conform for gain,
Or ftay the market of another reign.
Your broad-way fons wou'd never be too nice
To clofe with *Calvin*, if he paid their price;
But rais'd three fteeples high'r, wou'd change their note,
And quit the Caffock for the Canting-coat.
Now, if you damn this cenfure, as too bold,
Judge by your felves, and think not others fold.

Mean-time my fons accus'd, by fames report
Pay fmall attendance at the *Lyon's* court,
Nor rife with early crowds, nor flatter late,
(For filently they beg who daily wait.)

Prefer-

Preferment is beftow'd that comes unfought,
Attendance is a bribe, and then 'tis bought.
How they fhou'd fpeed, their fortune is untry'd,
For not to ask, is not to be deny'd.
For what they have, their *God* and *King* they blefs,
And hope they fhou'd not murmur, had they lefs.
But, if reduc'd fubfiftence to implore,
In common prudence they wou'd pafs your door;
Unpitty'd *Hudibrafs*; your-Champion friend,
Has fhown how far your charities extend.
This lafting verfe fhall on his tomb be read,
He fham'd you living, and upbraids you dead.

With odious *Atheift*-names you load your foes,
Your lib'ral *Clergy* why did I expofe?
It never fails in charities like thofe.
In climes where true religion is profefs'd,
That imputation were no laughing jeft.
But *Imprimatur*, with a Chaplain's name,
Is here fufficient licence to defame.

                     What

What wonder is't that black detraction thrives,
The Homicide of names is less than lives;
And yet the perjur'd murtherer survives.

    This said, she paus'd a little, and suppress'd
The boiling indignation of her breast;
She knew the vertue of her blade, nor wou'd
Pollute her satyr with ignoble bloud:
Her panting foes she saw before her lye,
And back she drew the shining weapon dry:
So when the gen'rous *Lyon* has in fight
His equal match, he rouses for the fight;
But when his foe lyes prostrate on the plain,
He sheaths his paws, uncurls his angry mane;
And, pleas'd with bloudless honours of the day,
Walks over, and disdains th' inglorious Prey,
So *JAMES*, if great with less we may compare,
Arrests his rowling thunder-bolts in air;
And grants ungratefull friends a lengthn'd space,
T'implore the remnants of long suff'ring grace.

                                 This

This breathing-time the *Matron* took; and then,
Refum'd the thrid of her difcourfe agen.
Be vengeance wholly left to powr's divine,
And let heav'n judge betwixt your fons and mine:
If joyes hereafter muft be purchas'd here
With lofs of all that mortals hold fo dear,
Then welcome infamy and publick fhame,
And, laft, a long farewell to worldly fame.
'Tis faid with eafe, but oh, how hardly try'd
By haughty fouls to humane honour ty'd !
O fharp convulfive pangs of agonizing pride !
Down then thou rebell, never more to rife,
And what thou didft, and do'ft fo dearly prize,
That fame, that darling fame, make that thy facrifice.
'Tis nothing thou haft giv'n, then add thy tears
For a long race of unrepenting years:
'Tis nothing yet; yet all thou haft to give,
Then add thofe *may-be* years thou haft to live.

N   Yet

Yet nothing ftill : then poor, and naked come,
Thy father will receive his unthrift home,
And thy bleft Saviour's bloud difcharge the mighty fum.

Thus (fhe purfu'd) I difcipline a fon
Whofe uncheck'd fury to revenge wou'd run:
He champs the bit, impatient of his lofs,
And ftarts a-fide, and flounders at the crofs.
Inftruct him better, gracious God, to know,
As thine is vengeance, fo forgivenefs too.
That fuff'ring from ill tongues he bears no more
Than what his Sovereign bears, and what his Saviour bore.

It now remains for you to fchool your child,
And ask why *God*'s anointed he revil'd ;
A *King* and *Princefs* dead ! did *Shimei* worfe ?
The curfer's punifhment fhould fright the curfe :
Your fon was warn'd, and wifely gave it o're,
But he who councell'd him, has paid the fcore :

The

The heavy malice cou'd no higher tend,

But wo to him on whom the weights defcend !

So to permitted ills the *Dæmon* flyes :

His rage is aim'd at him who rules the skyes ;

Conftrain'd to quit his caufe, no fuccour found,

The foe difcharges ev'ry Tyre around,

In clouds of fmoke abandoning the fight,

But his own thund'ring peals proclaim his flight.

In *Henry*'s change his charge as ill fucceeds,

To that long ftory little anfwer needs,

Confront but *Henry*'s words with *Henry*'s deeds.

Were fpace allow'd, with eafe it might be prov'd,

What fprings his bleffed reformation mov'd,

The dire effects appear'd in open fight,

Which from the caufe he calls a diftant flight,

And yet no larger leap than from the fun to light.

Now laft your fons a double *Pæan* found,

A *Treatife of Humility* is found.

'Tis

'Tis found, but better it had ne'er been fought
Than thus in Proteftant proceffion brought.
The fam'd original through *Spain* is known,
Rodriguez work, my celebrated fon,
Which yours, by ill-tranflating made his own;
Conceal'd its authour, and ufurp'd the name,
The bafeft and ignobleft theft of fame.
My Altars kindl'd firft that living coal,
Reftore, or practice better what you ftole:
That vertue could this humble verfe infpire,
'Tis all the reftitution I require.

Glad was the *Panther* that the charge was clos'd,
And none of all her fav'rite fons expos'd.
For laws of arms permit each injur'd man,
To make himfelf a fayer where he can.
Perhaps the plunder'd merchant cannot tell
The names of Pirates in whofe hands he fell:

But

But at the den of thieves he juſtly flies,

And ev'ry *Algerine* is lawfull prize.

No private perſon in the foes eſtate

Can plead exemption from the publick fate.

Yet Chriſtian laws allow not ſuch redreſs;

Then let the greater ſuperſede the leſs.

But let th' Abbetors of the *Panther*'s crime

Learn to make fairer wars another time.

Some characters may ſure be found to write

Among her ſons; for 'tis no common fight

A ſpotted Dam, and all her offspring white.

The *Salvage*, though ſhe ſaw her plea controll'd,

Yet wou'd not wholly ſeem to quit her hold,

But offer'd fairly to compound the ſtrife;

And judge converſion by the convert's life.

'Tis true, ſhe ſaid, I think it ſomewhat ſtrange.

So few ſhou'd follow profitable change;

For preſent joys are more to fleſh and bloud,

Than a dull proſpect of a diſtant good.

                                        'Twas

'Twas well alluded by a son of mine,

(I hope to quote him is not to purloin;)

Two magnets, heav'n and earth, allure to bliss;

The larger loadstone that, the nearer this:

The weak attraction of the greater fails,

We nodd a-while, but neighbourhood prevails:

But when the greater proves the nearer too,

I wonder more your converts come so slow.

Methinks in those who firm with me remain,

It shows a nobler principle than gain.

-Your inf'rence wou'd be strong (the *Hind* reply'd)

If yours were in effect the suff'ring side:

Your clergy sons their own in peace possess,

Nor are their prospects in reversion less.

My Proselytes are struck with awfull dread,

Your bloudy Comet-laws hang blazing o're their Head!

The respite they enjoy but onely lent,

The best they have to hope, protracted punishment.

Be judge your self, if int'reſt may prevail,
Which motives, yours or mine, will turn the ſcale.
While pride and pomp allure, and plenteous eaſe,
That is, till man's predominant paſſions ceaſe,
Admire no longer at my ſlow encreaſe.

By education moſt have been miſled,
So they believe, becauſe they ſo were bred.
The *Prieſt* continues what the nurſe began,
And thus the child impoſes on the man.
The reſt I nam'd before, nor need repeat :
But int'reſt is the moſt prevailing cheat,
The ſly ſeducer both of age and youth ;
They ſtudy that, and think they ſtudy truth :
When int'reſt fortifies an argument
Weak reaſon ſerves to gain the wills aſſent;
For ſouls, already warp'd, receive an eaſie bent.

Add long preſcription of eſtabliſh'd laws,
And picque of honour to maintain a cauſe,

And shame of change, and fear of future ill,
And Zeal, the blind conductor of the will;
And chief among the still mistaking crowd,
The fame of teachers obstinate and proud,
And more than all, the private Judge allow'd.
Disdain of Fathers which the daunce began,
And last, uncertain who's the narrower span,
The clown unread, and half-read gentleman.

To this the *Panther*, with a scornfull smile:
Yet still you travail with unwearied toil,
And range around the realm without controll
Among my sons, for Proselytes to prole,
And here and there you snap some silly soul.
You hinted fears of future change in state,
Pray heav'n you did not prophesie your fate;
Perhaps you think your time of triumph near,
But may mistake the season of the year;
The *Swallows* fortune gives you cause to fear.

For

For charity ('reply'd the Matron) tell
What fad mifchance thofe pretty birds befell.

Nay, no mifchance, (the falvage Dame reply'd)⎫
But want of wit in their unerring guide,   ⎬
And eager hafte, and gaudy hopes, and giddy pride.⎭
Yet, wifhing timely warning may prevail, .
Make you the moral, and I'll tell the tale.

The *Swallow*, privileg'd above the reft
Of all the birds, as man's familiar Gueft,
Purfues the Sun in fummer brisk and bold,
But wifely fhuns the perfecuting cold:
Is well to chancels and to chimnies known,
Though 'tis not thought fhe feeds on fmoak alone.
From hence fhe has been held of heav'nly line,
Endu'd with particles of foul divine.
This merry Chorifter had long poffefs'd
Her fummer feat, and feather'd well her neft:

O   Till

Till frowning skys began to change their chear
And time turn'd up the wrong fide of the year;
The fhedding trees began the ground to ftrow
With yellow leaves, and bitter blafts to blow.
Sad auguries of winter thence fhe drew,
Which by inftinct, or Prophecy, fhe knew:
When prudence warn'd her to remove betimes
And feek a better heav'n, and warmer clymes.

Her fons were fummon'd on a fteeples height,
And, call'd in common council, vote a flight;
The day was nam'd, the next that fhou'd be fair,
All to the gen'ral rendezvouz repair,
They try their flutt'ring wings, and truft themfelves in air.
But whether upward to the moon they go,
Or dream the winter out in caves below,
Or hawk at flies elfewhere, concerns not us to know.

Southwards, you may be fure, they bent their flight,
And harbour'd in a hollow rock at night:

Next

The Hind and the Panther.

Next morn they rofe and fet up ev'ry fail,
The wind was fair, but blew a *mackrel* gale :
The fickly young fat fhiv'ring on the fhoar,
Abhorr'd falt-water never feen before,
And pray'd their tender mothers to delay
The paffage, and expect a fairer day.

With thefe the *Martyn* readily concurr'd,
A church-begot, and church-believing bird ;
Of little body, but of lofty mind,
Round belly'd, for a dignity defign'd,
And much a dunce, as *Martyns* are by kind.
Yet often quoted 'Canon-laws, and *Code*,
And Fathers which he never underftood,
But little learning needs in noble bloud.
For, footh to fay, the *Swallow* brought him in,
Her houfhold Chaplain, and her next of kin.
In Superftition filly to excefs,
And cafting Schemes, by planetary guefs :

In fine, fhortwing'd, unfit himfelf to fly,
His fear foretold foul-weather in the sky.

Befides, a *Raven* from a wither'd Oak,
Left of their lodging, was obferv'd to croke.
That omen lik'd him not, fo his advice
Was prefent fafety, bought at any price:
(A feeming pious care, that cover'd cowardife.)
To ftrengthen this, he told a boding dream,
Of rifing waters, and a troubl'd ftream,
Sure figns of anguifh, dangers and diftrefs,
With fomething more, not lawfull to exprefs:
By which he flyly feem'd to intimate
Some fecret revelation of their fate.
For he concluded, once upon a time,
He found a leaf infcrib'd with facred rime,
Whofe antique characters did well denote
The *Sibyl's* hand of the *Cumæan* Grott:
The mad Divinerefs had plainly writ,
A time fhould come (but many ages yet,)

In.

In which, finifter deftinies ordain,
A *Dame* fhou'd drown with all her feather'd train,
And feas from thence be call'd the*Chelidonian* main.
At this, fome fhook for fear, the more devout
Arofe, and blefs'd themfelves from head to foot.

'Tis true, fome ftagers of the wifer fort
Made all thefe idle wonderments their fport:
They faid, their onely danger was delay,
And he who heard what ev'ry fool cou'd fay,
Wou'd never fix his thoughts, but trim his time away.
The paffage yet was good, the wind, 'tis true,
Was fomewhat high, but that was nothing new,
Nor more than ufual *Equinoxes* blew.
The Sun (already from the fcales declin'd)
Gave little hopes of better days behind,
But change from bad to worfe of weather and of wind.
Nor need they fear the dampnefs of the Sky
Should flag their wings, and hinder them to fly,
'Twas onely water thrown on fails too dry.

But.

But, leaft of all *Philofophy* prefumes

Of truth in dreams, from melancholy fumes :

Perhaps the *Martyn* hous'd in holy ground,

Might think of Ghofts that walk their midnight round,

Till groffer atoms tumbling in the ftream

Of fancy, madly met and clubb'd into a dream.

As little weight his vain prefages bear,

Of ill effect to fuch alone who fear.

Moft prophecies are of a piece with thefe,

Each *Noftradamus* can foretell with eafe:

Not naming perfons, and confounding times,

One cafual truth fupports a thoufand lying rimes.

Th' advice was true, but fear had feiz'd the moft,

And all good counfel is on cowards loft.

The queftion crudely put, to fhun delay,

'Twas carry'd by the *major* part to ftay.

His point thus gain'd, Sir *Martyn* dated thence

His pow'r, and from a Prieft became a Prince.

He

He order'd all things with a bufie care,

And cells, and refeétories did prepare,

And large provifions laid of winter fare.

But now and then let fall a word or two

Of hope, that heav'n fome miracle might fhow,

And, for their fakes, the fun fhou'd backward go ;

Againft the laws of nature upward climb,

And, mounted on the *Ram*, renew the prime :

For which two proofs in Sacred ftory lay,

Of *Ahaz* dial, and of *Jofhuah's* day.

In expeétation of fuch times as thefe

A chapel hous'd 'em, truly call'd of eafe :

For *Martyn* much devotion did not ask,

They pray'd fometimes, and that was all their task.

It happen'd (as beyond the reach of wit

Blind prophecies may have a lucky hit)

That, this accomplifh'd, or at leaft in part,

Gave great repute to their new *Merlin's* art.

Some.

Some * *Swifts*, the Gyants of the *Swallow* kind,　*Otherwise call'd Martlets.*
Large limb'd, ftout-hearted, but of ftupid mind,
(For *Swiffes*, or for *Gibeonites* defign'd,)
Thefe Lubbers, peeping through a broken pane,
To fuck frefh air furvey'd the neighbouring plain ;
And faw (but fcarcely could believe their eyes)
New Bloffoms flourifh, and new flow'rs arife ;
As God had been abroad, and walking there,
Had left his foot-fteps, and reform'd the year :
The funny hills from far were feen to glow
With glittering beams, and in the meads below
The burnifh'd brooks appear'd with liquid gold to flow.
At laft they heard the foolifh *Cuckow* fing,
Whofe note proclaim'd the holy-day of fpring.

No longer doubting, all prepare to fly,
And repoffefs their patrimonial fky.
The *Prieft* before 'em did his wings difplay ;
And, that good omens might attend their way,
As luck wou'd have it, 'twas St. *Martyn's* day.

Who

Who but the *Swallow* now triumphs alone,
The Canopy of heaven is all her own,
Her youthfull offspring to their haunts repair ;
And glide along in glades, and skim in air,
And dip for infects in the purling springs,
And ftoop on rivers to refrefh their wings.
Their mothers think a fair provifion made,
That ev'ry fon can live upon his trade,
And now the carefull charge is off their hands,
Look out for husbands, and new nuptial bands :
The youthfull widow longs to be fupply'd ;
But firft the lover is by Lawyers ty'd
To fettle jointure-chimneys on the bride.
So thick they couple, in fo fhort a fpace,
That *Martyns* marr'age offrings rife apace ;
Their ancient houfes, running to decay,
Are furbifh'd up, and cemented with clay ;
They teem already ; ftore of eggs are laid,
And brooding mothers call *Lucina's* aid.

P   Fame

Fame fpreads the news, and foreign fowls appear
In flocks to greet the new returning year,
To blefs the founder, and partake the cheer.

And now 'twas time (fo faft their numbers rife)
To plant abroad, and people colonies;
The youth drawn forth, as *Martyn* had defir'd,
(For fo their cruel deftiny requir'd)
Were fent far off on an ill fated day;
The reft wou'd need conduct 'em on their way,
And *Martyn* went, becaufe he fear'd alone to ftay.

So long they flew, with inconfiderate hafte
That now their afternoon began to wafte;
And, what was ominous, that very morn
The Sun was entr'd into *Capricorn*;
Which, by their bad Aftronomers account,
That week the virgin balance fhou'd remount;
An infant moon eclips'd him in his way,
And hid the fmall remainders of his day.

The

The crow'd amaz'd, pursu'd no certain mark ;
But birds met birds, and justled in the dark ;
Few mind the publick in a Panick fright ;
And fear increas'd the horrour of the night.
Night came, but unattended with repose,
Alone she came; no sleep their eyes to close,
Alone, and black she came, no friendly stars arose.

What shou'd they doe, beset with dangers round,
No neighb'ring Dorp, no lodging to be found,
But bleaky plains, and bare unhospitable ground.
The latter brood, who just began to fly
Sick-feather'd, and unpractis'd in the sky,
For succour to their helpless mother call,
She spread her wings; some few beneath 'em craul,
She spread 'em wider yet, but cou'd not cover all.
T'augment their woes, the winds began to move
Debate in air, for empty fields above,
Till *Boreas* got the skyes, and powr'd amain
His ratling hail-stones mix'd with snow and rain.

The

The joyleſs morning late aroſe, and found
A dreadfull deſolation reign a-round,
Some buried in the Snow, ſome frozen to the ground:
The reſt were ſtrugling ſtill with death, and lay
The *Crows* and *Ravens* rights, an undefended prey;
Excepting *Martyn's* race, for they and he
Had gain'd the ſhelter of a hollow tree,
But ſoon diſcover'd by a ſturdy clown,
He headed all the rabble of a town,
And finiſh'd 'em with bats, or poll'd 'em down.
Martyn himſelf was caught a-live, and try'd
For treas'nous crimes, becauſe the laws provide
No *Martyn* there in winter ſhall abide.
High on an Oak which never leaf ſhall bear,
He breath'd his laſt, expos'd to open air,
And there his corps, unbleſs'd, are hanging ſtill,
To ſhow the change of winds with his prophetick bill.

The

The patience of the *Hind* did almoſt fail,
For well ſhe mark'd the malice of the tale :
Which Ribbald art their church to *Luther* owes, ⎞
In malice it began, by malice grows, ⎬
He ſow'd the *Serpent*'s teeth, an iron-harveſt roſe. ⎠
But moſt in *Martyn*'s character and fate, ⎞
She ſaw her ſlander'd ſons, the *Panther*'s hate, ⎬
The people's rage, the perſecuting ſtate : ⎠
Then ſaid, I take th' advice in friendly part,
You clear your conſcience, or at leaſt your heart :
Perhaps you fail'd in your fore-ſeeing skill,
For *Swallows* are unlucky birds to kill :
As for my ſons, the family is bleſs'd,
Whoſe ev'ry child is equal to the reſt :
No church reform'd can boaſt a blameleſs line ;
Such *Martyns* build in yours, and more than mine :
Or elſe an old fanatick Authour lyes
Who ſumm'd their Scandals up by Centuries.

But, through your parable I plainly fee
The bloudy laws, the crowds barbarity:
The fun-fhine that offends the purblind fight,
Had fome their wifhes, it wou'd foon be night.
Miftake me not, the charge concerns not you,
Your fons are male-contents, but yet are true,
As far as non-refiftance makes 'em fo,
But that's a word of neutral fenfe you know,
A paffive term which no relief will bring,
But trims betwixt a rebell and a king.

    Reft well affur'd, the *Pardalis* reply'd,
My fons wou'd all fupport the regal fide,
Though heav'n forbid the caufe by battel fhou'd be try'd.

    The Matron anfwer'd with a loud Amen,
And thus purfu'd her argument agen.
If as you fay, and as I hope no lefs,
Your fons will practife what your felf profefs,
What angry pow'r prevents our prefent peace?

                    The

The *Lyon*, ftudious of our common good;
Defires, (and Kings defires are ill withftood,)
To join our Nations in a lafting love;
The barrs betwixt are eafie to remove,
For fanguinary laws were never made above
If you condemn that Prince of Tyranny
Whofe mandate forc'd your *Gallick* friends to fly,
Make not a worfe example of your own,
Or ceafe to rail at caufelefs rigour-fhown,
And let the guiltlefs perfon throw the ftone.
His blunted fword, your fuff'ring brotherhood
Have feldom felt, he ftops it fhort of bloud :
But you have ground the perfecuting knife,
And fet it to a razor edge on life.
Curs'd be the wit which cruelty refines,
Or to his father's rod the *Scorpion* joins;
Your finger is more grofs than the great Monarch's loins.
But you perhaps remove that bloudy note,
And ftick it on the firft Reformers coat.

Oh

Oh let their crime in long oblivion sleep,
'Twas theirs indeed to make, 'tis yours to keep.
Unjuft, or juft, is all the queftion now,
'Tis plain, that not repealing you allow.

To name the Teft wou'd put you in a rage,
You charge not that on any former age,
But fmile to think how innocent you ftand
Arm'd by a weapon put into your hand.
Yet ftill remember that you weild a fword
Forg'd by your foes againft your Sovereign Lord.
Defign'd to hew th' imperial Cedar down,
Defraud Succeffion, and dif-heir the Crown.
T' abhor the makers, and their laws approve,
Is to hate Traytors, and the treafon love.
What means it elfe, which now your children fay,
We made it not, nor will we take away.

Suppofe

Suppofe fome great Oppreffor had by flight
Of law, diffeis'd your brother of his right,
Your common fire furrendring in a fright;
Would you to that unrighteous title ftand,
Meft by the villain's will to heir the land?
More juft was *Judas*, who his Saviour fold;
The facrilegious bribe he cou'd not hold,
Nor hang in peace,before he rendr'd back the gold.
What more could you have done,than now you doe,
Had *Oates* and *Bedlow*, and their Plot been true?
Some fpecious reafons for thofe wrongs were found;
The dire Magicians threw their mifts around,
And wife men walk'd as on inchanted ground.
But now when time has made th' impofture plain,
(Late though he follow'd truth, & limping held her train,)
What new delufion charms your cheated eyes again?
The painted Harlot might awhile bewitch,
But why the Hag uncas'd, and all obfcene with itch?

Q   The

The firſt Reformers were a modeſt race,
Our Peers poſſeſs'd in peace their native place :
And when rebellious arms o'return'd the ſtate,
They ſuffer'd onely in the common fate ;
But now the Sov'reign mounts the regal chair
And mitr'd ſeats are full, yet *David*'s bench is bare :
Your anſwer is, they were not diſpoſſeſs'd,
They need but rub their mettle on the Teſt
To prove their ore : 'twere well if gold alone
Were touch'd and try'd on your diſcerning ſtone ;
But that unfaithfull Teſt, unfound will paſs
The droſs of Atheiſts, and ſectarian braſs :
As if th' experiment were made to hold
For baſe productions, and reject the gold :
Thus men ungodded may to places riſe,
And ſects may be preferr'd without diſguiſe :
No danger to the church or ſtate from theſe,
The Papiſt onely has his Writ of eaſe.

No gainfull office gives him the pretence
To grind the Subject or defraud the Prince.
Wrong confcience, or no confcience may deferve
To thrive, but ours alone is privileg'd to fterve.

Still thank your felves you cry, your noble race
We banifh not, but they forfake the place.
Our doors are open: true, but e'er they come,
You tofs your cenfing Teft, and fume the room';
As if 'twere *Toby's* rival to expell,
And fright the fiend who could not bear the fmell.

To this the *Panther* fharply had reply'd,
But, having gain'd a Verdict on her fide,
She wifely gave the lofer leave to chide;
Well fatisfy'd to have the But and peace,
And for the Plaintiff's caufe fhe car'd the lefs,
Becaufe fhe fu'd in *formâ Pauperis* ;
Yet thought it decent fomething fhou'd be faid,
For fecret guilt by filence is betray'd:

So neither granted all, nor much deny'd,
But anfwer'd with a yawning kind of pride.

Methinks fuch terms of proferr'd peace you bring
As once *Æneas* to th' *Italian* King :
By long poffeffion all the land is mine, .
You ftrangers come with your intruding line,
To fhare my fceptre, which you call to join.
You plead like him an ancient Pedigree, .
And claim a peacefull feat by fates decree.
In ready pomp your Sacrificer ftands,
T'unite the *Trojan* and the *Latin* bands,
And that the League more firmly may be ty'd,
Demand the fair *Lavinia* for your bride.
Thus plaufibly you veil th' intended wrong,
But ftill you bring your exil'd gods along ;
And will endeavour in fucceeding fpace,
Thofe houfhold Poppits on our hearths to place.
Perhaps fome barb'rous laws have been preferr'd,
I fpake againft the *Teft*, but was not heardi ;

Thefe to refcind, and Peerage to reftore,
My gracious Sov'reign wou'd my vote implore:
I owe him much, but owe my confcience more.

    Confcience is then your Plea, reply'd the Dame,
Which well-inform'd will ever be the fame.
But yours is much of the *Camelion* hew,
To change the dye with ev'ry diff'rent view.
When firft the *Lyon* fat with awfull fway
Your confcience taught you duty to obey:
He might have had your Statutes and your Teft,
No confcience but of fubjects was profefs'd.
He found your temper, and no farther try'd,
But on that broken reed your church rely'd.
In vain the fects affay'd their utmoft art
With offer'd treafure to efpoufe their part,
Their treafures were a bribe too mean to move his heart.
But when by long experience you had proov'd,
How far he cou'd forgive, how well he lov'd;

A good-

A goodnefs that excell'd his godlike race,
And onely fhort of heav'ns unbounded grace:
A floud of mercy that o'erflow'd our Ifle,
Calm in the rife, and fruitfull as the *Nile*,
Forgetting whence your *Ægypt* was fupply'd,
You thought your Sov'reign bound to fend the tide:
Nor upward look'd on that immortal fpring,
But vainly deem'd, he durft not be a king :
Then confcience, unreftrain'd by fear, began
To ftretch her limits, and extend the fpan,
Did his indulgence as her gift difpofe,
And made a wife Alliance with her foes.
Can confcience own th' affociating name,
And raife no blufhes to conceal her fhame ?
For fure fhe has been thought a bafhfull Dame.
But if the caufe by battel fhou'd be try'd,
You grant fhe muft efpoufe the regal fide :
O *Proteus* Confcience, never to be ty'd !
What *Phœbus* from the *Tripod* fhall difclofe,
Which are in laft refort, your friends or foes ?

                                        Homer,

Homer, who learn'd the language of the sky,
The feeming *Gordian* knot wou'd foon unty;
Immortal pow'rs the term of confcience know,
But int'reft is her name with men below.

Confcience or int'reft be't, or both in one ;
(The *Panther* anfwer'd in a furly tone,)
The firft commands me to maintain the Crown,
The laft forbids to throw my barriers down.
Our penal laws no fons of yours admit,
Our *Teft* excludes your Tribe from benefit.
Thefe are my banks your ocean to withftand,
Which proudly rifing overlooks the land:
And once let in, with unrefifted fway
Wou'd fweep the Paftors and their flocks away.
Think not my judgment leads me to comply
With laws unjuft, but hard neceffity :
Imperious need which cannot be withftood
Makes ill authentick, for a greater good.

Poffefs

Possess your soul with patience, and attend :
A more auspicious Planet may ascend ;
Good fortune may present some happier time,
With means to cancell my unwilling crime ;
(Unwilling, witness all ye Pow'rs above)
To mend my errours and redeem your love :
That little space you safely may allow,
Your all-dispensing pow'r protects you now.

Hold, said the *Hind,* 'tis needless to explain ;
You wou'd *postpone* me to another reign :
Till when you are content to be unjust,
Your part is to possess, and mine to trust.
A fair exchange propos'd of future chance,
For present profit and inheritance :
Few words will serve to finish our dispute,
Who will not now repeal wou'd persecute ;
To ripen green revenge your hopes attend,
Wishing that happier Planet wou'd ascend :

For

For fhame let Confcience be your Plea no more,
To will hereafter, proves fhe might before ;
But fhe's a Bawd to gain, and holds the Door.

Your care about your Banks, infers a fear
Of threatning Floods, and Inundations near ;
If fo, a juft Reprife would only be
Of what the Land ufurp'd upon the Sea ;
And all your Jealoufies but ferve to fhow
Your Ground is, like your Neighbour-Nation, low.
T' intrench in what you grant unrighteous Laws,
Is to diftruft the juftice of your Caufe;
And argues that the true Religion lyes
In thofe weak Adverfaries you defpife.

Tyrannick force is that which leaft you fear,
The found is frightfull in a Chriftian's ear ;
Avert it, Heav'n; nor let that Plague be fent
To us from the difpeopled Continent.

R   But

But Piety commands me to refrain;
Thofe Pray'rs are needlefs in this Monarch's Reign.
Behold ! how he protects your Friends oppreft,
Receives the Banifh'd, fuccours the Diftrefs'd:
Behold, for you may read an honeft open Breaft.
He ftands in Day-light, and difdains to hide
An Act to which, by Honour he is ty'd,
A generous, laudable, and Kingly Pride.
Your Teft he would repeal, his Peers reftore,
This when he fays he means, he means no more.

Well, faid the *Panther*, I believe him juft,
And yet——

And yet, 'tis but becaufe you muft,
You would be trufted, but you would not truft.
The *Hind* thus briefly; and difdain'd t' inlarge
On Pow'r of *Kings*, and their Superiour charge,

As Heav'ns Truftees before the Peoples choice:
Tho' fure the *Panther* did not much rejoyce
To hear thofe *Echo's* giv'n of her once Loyal voice.

The *Matron* woo'd her Kindnefs to the laft,
But cou'd not win ; her hour of Grace was paft.
Whom, thus perfifting, when fhe could not bring
To leave the *Woolf*, and to believe her King,
She gave Her up, and fairly wifh'd her Joy
Of her late Treaty with her new Ally :
Which well fhe hop'd wou'd more fuccefsfull prove,
Than was the *Pigeons*, and the *Buzzards* love.
The *Panther* ask'd, what concord there cou'd be
Betwixt two kinds whofe Natures difagree ?
The *Dame* reply'd, 'Tis fung in ev'ry Street,
The common chat of Goffips when they meet:
But, fince unheard by you, 'tis worth your while
To take a wholefome Tale, tho' told in homely ftile.

A Plain good Man, whofe Name is underftood,
(So few deferve the name of Plain and Good)
Of three fair lineal Lordfhips ftood poffefs'd,
And liv'd, as reafon was, upon the beft ;
Inur'd to hardfhips from his early Youth,
Much had he done, and fuffer'd for his truth :
At Land, and Sea, in many a doubtfull Fight,
Was never known a more adven'trous Knight,
Who oftner drew his Sword,and always for the right.

  As fortune wou'd (his fortune came tho' late)
He took Poffeffion of his juft Eftate :
Nor rack'd his Tenants with increafe of Rent,
Nor liv'd too fparing, nor too largely fpent ;
But overlook'd his *Hinds*, their Pay was juft,
And ready, for he fcorn'd to go on truft :
Slow to refolve, but in performance quick;
So true, that he was awkard at a trick.

                                        For

For little Souls on little fhifts rely,

And coward Arts of mean Expedients try: .

The noble Mind will dare do any thing but lye.

Falfe Friends, (his deadlieft foes,) could find no way

But fhows of honeft bluntnefs to betray ;

That unfufpected plainnefs he believ'd ;

He look'd into Himfelf, and was deceiv'd.

Some lucky Planet fure attends his Birth,

Or Heav'n wou'd make a Miracle on Earth ;

For profp'rous Honefty is feldom feen :

To bear fo dead a weight, and yet to win.

It looks as Fate with Nature's Law would ftrive,

To fhew Plain dealing once an age may thrive:

And, when fo tough a frame fhe could not bend,

Exceeded her Commiffion to befriend.

This gratefull man, as Heav'n encreas'd his Store,

Gave *God* again, and daily fed his Poor ;

His Houfe with all convenience was purvey'd ;

The reft he found, but rais'd the Fabrick where he pray'd ;

And

And in that Sacred Place, his beauteous Wife
Employ'd Her happieſt hours of Holy Life.

Nor did their Alms extend to thoſe alone
Whom common Faith more ſtrictly made their own;
A ſort of *Doves* were hous'd too near their Hall,
Who croſs the Proverb, and abound with Gall.
Tho' ſome 'tis true, are paſſively inclin'd,
The greater Part degenerate from their kind;
Voracious Birds, that hotly Bill and breed,
And largely drink, becauſe on Salt they feed.
Small Gain from them their Bounteous Owner draws;
Yet, bound by Promiſe, he ſupports their Cauſe,
As Corporations priviledg'd by Laws.

That Houſe which harbour to their kind affords
Was built, long ſince, God knows, for better Birds;
But flutt'ring there they neſtle near the Throne,
And lodge in Habitations not their own,
By their high Crops, and Corny Gizzards known.

Like

Like *Harpy's* they could fcent a plenteous board,

Then to be fure they never fail'd their Lord.

The reft was form, and bare Attendance paid,

They drunk, and eat, and grudgingly obey'd.

The more they fed, they raven'd ftill for more,

They drain'd from *Dan*, and left *Beerjheba* poor;

All this they had by Law, and none repin'd,

The pref'rence was but due to *Levi's* Kind,

But when fome Lay-preferment fell by chance

The Gourmands made it their Inheritance.

When once poffefs'd, they never quit their Claim,

For then 'tis fanctify'd to Hea'vens high Name;

And Hallow'd thus they cannot give Confent,

The Gift fhould be prophan'd by Wordly management.

Their Flefh was never to the Table ferv'd,

Tho' 'tis not thence inferr'd the Birds were ftarv'd;

But that their Mafter did not like the Food,

As rank, and breeding Melancholy Blood.

As.

Nor did it with His Gracious Nature fuite,

Ev'n tho' they were not Doves, to perfecute :

Yet He refus'd, (nor could they take Offence)

Their Glutton Kind fhould teach him abftinence.

Nor Confecrated Grain their Wheat he thought,

Which new from treading in their Bills they brought :

But left his Hinds, each in his Private Pow'r,

That thofe who like the Bran might leave the Flow'r.

He for himfelf, and not for others chofe,

Nor would He be impos'd on, nor impofe ;

But in their Faces His Devotion paid,

And Sacrifice with Solemn Rites was made,

And Sacred Incenfe on His Altars laid.

Befides thefe jolly Birds, whofe Crops impure,

Repay'd their Commons with their Salt Manure ;

Another Farm he had behind his Houfe,

Not overftock't, but barely for his ufe ;

Wherein his poor Domeftick Poultry fed,

And from His Pious Hands receiv'd their Bread.

Our

Our pamper'd Pigeons with malignant Eyes,

Beheld thefe Inmates, and their Nurferies:

Tho' hard their fare, at Ev'ning, and at Morn

A Cruife of Water and an Ear of Corn;

Yet ftill they grudg'd that Modicum, and thought

A Sheaf in ev'ry fingle Grain was brought;

Fain would they filch that little Food away,

While unreftrain'd thofe happy Gluttons prey.

And much they griev'd to fee fo nigh their Hall,

The Bird that warn'd St. *Peter* of his Fall;

That he fhould raife his miter'd Creft on high,

And clap his Wings, and call his Family

To Sacred Rites; and vex th' Etherial Pow'rs

With midnight Mattins, at uncivil Hours:

Nay more, his quiet Neighbours fhould moleft,

Juft in the fweetnefs of their Morning reft.

Beaft of a Bird, fupinely when he might

Lye fnugg and fleep, to rife before the light:

What if his dull Forefathers us'd that cry;

Cou'd he not let a Bad Example dye?

The VVorld was fall'n into an eafier way;

This Age knew better, than to Faft and Pray.

Good Senfe in Sacred VVorfhip would appear

So to begin, as they might end the year.

Such feats in former times had wrought the falls

Of crowing Chanticleers in Cloyfter'd VValls.

Expell'd for this, and for their Lands they fled;

And Sifter Partlet with her hooded head

Was hooted hence, becaufe fhe would not pray a Bed.

The way to win the reftiff, World to God,

Was to lay by the Difciplining Rod,

Unnatural Fafts, and Foreign Forms of Pray'r;

Religion frights us with a meen fevere.

'Tis Prudence to reform her into Eafe,

And put Her in Undrefs to make Her pleas:

A lively Faith will bear aloft the Mind,

And leave the Luggage of Good VVorks behind.

Such

Such Doctrines in the Pigeon-houfe were taught,
You need not ask how wondroufly they wrought;
But fure the common Cry was all for thefe
Whofe Life, and Precept both encourag'd Eafe.
Yet fearing thofe alluring Baits might fail,
And Holy Deeds o're all their Arts prevail :
(For Vice, tho' frontlefs, and of harden'd Face
Is daunted at the fight of awfull Grace)
An hideous Figure of their Foes they drew,
Nor Lines, nor Looks, nor Shades, nor Colours true ;
And this Grotefque defign, expos'd to Publick view.
One would have thought it fome Ægyptian Piece,
With Garden-Gods, and barking Deities,
More thick than *Ptolomey* has ftuck the Skies.
All fo perverfe a Draught, fo far unlike,
It was no Libell where it meant to ftrike :
Yet ftill the daubing pleas'd, and Great and Small
To view the Monfter crowded Pigeon-hall.

There Chanticleer was drawn upon his knees.
Adoring Shrines, and Stocks of Sainted Trees,
And by him, a mifhapen, ugly Race;
The Curfe of God was feen on ev'ry Face:
No *Holland* Emblem could that Malice mend,
But ftill the worfe the look the fitter for a Fiend.

The Mafter of the Farm difpleas'd to find
So much of Rancour in fo mild a kind,
Enquir'd into the Caufe, and came to know;
The Paffive Church had ftruck the foremoft blow :
VVith groundlefs Fears, and Jealoufies poffeft,
As if this troublefome intruding Gueft
VVould drive the Birds of *Venus*, from their Neft.
A Deed his inborn Equity abhorr'd;
But Int'reft will not truft, tho God fhould plight his Word.

A Law, the Source of many Future harms,
Had banifh'd all the Poultry from the Farms ;

With

With lofs of Life, if any fhould be found

To crow or peck on this forbidden Ground.

That Bloody Statute chiefly was defign'd·

For *Chanticleer* the white, of Clergy kind ;

But after-malice did not long forget

The Lay that wore the Robe, and Coronet ;

For them, for their Inferiours and Allyes,

Their Foes a deadly *Shibboleth* devife :

By which unrighteoufly it was decreed,

That none to Truft, or Profit fhould fucceed,

Who would not fwallow firft a poyfonous wicked Weed:

Or that, to which old *Socrates* was curs't,

Or Henbane-Juice to fwell 'em till they burft,

The Patron (as in reafon) thought it hard

To fee this Inquifition in his Yard,

By which the Soveraign was of Subjects ufe debarr'd.

All gentle means he try'd, which might withdraw.

Th' Effects of fo unnatural a Law :

But

But ſtill the Dove-houſe obſtinately ſtood
Deaf to their own, and to their Neighbours good:
And which was worſe, (if any worſe could be)
Repented of their boaſted Loyalty :
Now made the Champions of a cruel Cauſe,
And drunk with Fumes of Popular Applauſe ;
For thoſe whom God to ruine has deſign'd,
He fits for Fate, and firſt deſtroys their Mind.

New Doubts indeed they daily ſtrove to raiſe,
Suggeſted Dangers, interpos'd Delays;
And Emiſſary Pigeons had in ſtore,
Such as the *Meccan* Prophet us'd of yore,
To whiſper Counſels in their Patrons Ear;
And veil'd their falſe Advice with Zealous Fear.
The Maſter ſmil'd to ſee 'em work in vain,
To wear him out, and make an idle reign :
He ſaw, but ſuffer'd their Protractive Arts,
And ſtrove by mildneſs to reduce their Hearts;

But

But they abus'd that Grace to make Allyes,
And fondly clos'd with former Enemies;
For Fools are double Fools, endeav'ring to be wife.

After a grave Confult what courfe were beft,
One more mature in Folly than the reft,
Stood up, and told 'em, with his head afide,
That defp'rate Cures muft be to defp'rate Ills apply'd:
And therefore fince their main impending fear
Was from th' encreafing race of *Chanticleer* :
Some Potent Bird of Prey they ought to find,
A Foe profefs'd to him, and all his kind:
Some haggar'd *Hawk*, who had her eyry nigh,
Well pounc'd to faften, and well wing'd to fly ;
One they might truft, their common wrongs to wreak:
The *Mufquet*, and the *Coyftrel* were too weak,
Too fierce the *Falcon*, but above the reft,
The noble *Buzzard* ever pleas'd me beft;
Of fmall Renown, 'tis true, for not to lye,
We call him but a *Hawk* by courtefie.

I

I know he haunts the *Pigeon*-Houfe and Farm,

And more, in time of War, has done us harm;

But all his hate on trivial Points depends,

Give up our Forms, and we fhall foon be friends.

For *Pigeons* flefh he feems not much to care,

Cram'd *Chickens* are a more delicious fare;

On this high Potentate, without delay,

I wifh you would conferr the Sovereign fway :

Petition him t' accept the Government,

And let a fplendid Embaffy be fent.

This pithy Speech prevail'd, and all agreed,

Old Enmity's forgot, the *Buzzard* fhould fucceed.

Their welcom Suit was granted foon as heard,

His Lodgings furnifh'd, and a Train prepar'd,

With *B's* upon their Breaft, appointed for his Guard.

He came, and Crown'd with great Solemnity,

God fave King *Buzzard*, was the gen'rall cry.

As

A Portly Prince, and goodly to the fight,
He feem'd a Son of *Anach* for his height :
Like thofe whom ftature did to Crowns prefer ;
Black-brow'd, and bluff, like *Homer's Jupiter* :
Broad-back'd, and Brawny built for Loves delight,
A Prophet form'd, to make a female Profelyte.
A Theologue more by need, than genial bent,
By Breeding fharp, by Nature confident.
Int'reft in all his Actions was difcern'd ;
More learn'd than Honeft, more a Wit than learn'd.
Or forc'd by Fear, or by his Profit led,
Or both conjoyn'd, his Native clime he fled :
But brought the Vertues of his Heav'n along;
A fair Behaviour, and a fluent Tongue.
And yet with all his Arts he could not thrive ;
The moft unlucky Parafite alive.
Loud Praifes to prepare his Paths he fent,
And then himfelf purfu'd his Compliment :

T   But

But, by reverſe of Fortune chac'd away,

His Gifts no longer than their Author ſtay :

He ſhakes the Duſt againſt th' ungrateful race,

And leaves the ſtench of Ordures in the place.

Oft has he flatter'd, and blaſphem'd the ſame,

For in his Rage, he ſpares no Sov'rains name :

The Hero, and the Tyrant change their ſtyle

By the ſame meaſure that they frown or ſmile ;

When well receiv'd by hoſpitable Foes,

The kindneſs he returns, is to expoſe :

For Courteſies, tho'. undeſerv'd and great,

No gratitude in Fellon-minds beget,

As tribute to his VVit, the churl receives the treat.

His praiſe of Foes is venemouſly Nice,.

So touch'd, it turns a Vertue to a Vice :

A Greek, and bountiful foreyarns us twice.

Sev'n Sacraments he wiſely do's diſown,

Becauſe he knows Confeſſion ſtands for one ;

Where Sins to ſacred ſilence are convey'd,

And not for Fear, or Love, to be betray'd :

But

But he, uncall'd, his Patron to controul,
Divulg'd the secret whispers of his Soul:
Stood forth th' accusing Sathan of his Crimes,
And offer'd to the *Moloch* of the Times.
Prompt to assayle, and carelefs of defence,
Invulnerable in his Impudence;
He dares the VVorld, and eager of a name,
He thrusts about, and justles into fame.
Frontlefs, and Satyr-proof he scowr's the streets,
And runs an *Indian* muck at all he meets.
So fond of loud Report, that not to mifs
Of being known (his laft and utmoft blifs)
He rather would be known, for what he is.

Such was, and is the Captain of the teft,
Tho' half his Vertues are not here exprefs't;
The modefty of Fame conceals the reft.
The fpleenful *Pigeons* never could create
A Prince more profert to revenge their hate.

Indeed,

Indeed, more proper to revenge, than fave;
A King, whom in his wrath, th' Almighty gave:
For all the Grace the Landlord had allow'd,
But made the *Buzzard* and the *Pigeons* proud;
Gave time to fix their Friends, and to feduce the crowd.
They long their Fellow-Subjects to inthrall,
Their Patrons promife into queftion call,
And vainly think he meant to make 'em Lords of all.

Falfe Fears their Leaders fail'd not to fuggeft,
As if the *Doves* were to be difpoffeft;
Nor Sighs, nor Groans, nor gogling Eyes did want;
For now the *Pigeons* too had learn'd to Cant.
The Houfe of Pray'r is ftock'd with large encreafe;
Nor Doors, nor Windows can contain the Prefs;
For Birds of ev'ry feather fill th' abode;
Ev'n Atheifts out of envy own a God:
And reeking from the Stews, Adult'rers come;
Like *Goths* and *Vandals* to demolifh *Rome*.

That

That Confcience which to all their Crimes was mute,
Now calls aloud, and cryes to Perfecute.
No rigour of the Laws to be releas'd,
And much the lefs, becaufe it was their Lords requeft:
They thought it great their Sov'rain to controul,
And nam'd their Pride, Nobility of Soul.

'Tis true, the *Pigeons,* and their Prince Elect
Were fhort of Pow'r their purpofe to effect:
But with their Quills, did all the hurt they cou'd,
And cuff'd the tender *Chickens* from their food:
And much the *Buzzard* in their Caufe did ftir,
Tho' naming not the Patron, to infer
With all refpect, He was a grofs Idolater.
   But when th' Imperial owner did efpy
That thus they turn'd his Grace to villany,
Not fuff'ring wrath to difcompofe his mind,
He ftrove a temper for th' extreams to find,
So to be juft, as he might ftill be kind.

Then,

Then, all Maturely weigh'd, pronounc'd a Doom
Of Sacred Strength for ev'ry Age to come.
By this the Doves their Wealth and State possess,
No Rights infring'd, but Licence to oppress:
Such Pow'r have they as Factious Lawyers long
To Crowns ascrib'd, that Kings can do no wrong:
But, since His own Domestick Birds have try'd
The dire Effects of their destructive Pride,
He deems that Proof a Measure to the rest,
Concluding well within his Kingly Breast,
His Fowl of Nature too unjustly were opprest.
He therefore makes all Birds of ev'ry Sect
Free of his Farm, with promise to respect
Their sev'ral Kinds alike, and equally protect.
His Gracious Edict the same Franchise yields
To all the wild Encrease of Woods and Fields,
And who in Rocks aloof, and who in Steeples builds.
To *Crows* the like Impartial Grace affords,
And *Choughs* and *Daws*, and such Republick Birds:

Secur'd

Secur'd with ample Priviledge to feed,
Each has his Diftrict, and his Bounds decreed :
Combin'd in common Int'reft with his own,
But not to pafs the Pigeons *Rubicon.*

Here ends the Reign of this pretended Dove ;
All Prophecies accomplifh'd from above,
For *Shiloh* comes the Scepter to Remove.
Reduc'd from Her Imperial High Abode,
Like *Dyonyfius* to a private Rod.:
The Paffive Church, that with pretended Grace
Did Her diftinctive Mark in Duty place,
Now Touch'd, Reviles Her Maker to his Face.

What after happen'd is not hard to guefs ;
The fmall Beginnings had a large Encreafe,
And Arts and Wealth fucceed (the fecret fpoils of Peace.)
'Tis faid the Doves repented, tho' too late,
Become the Smiths of their own Foolifh Fate:

Nor

Nor did their Owner haften their ill hour:
But, funk in Credit,they decreas'd in Pow'r:
Like Snows in warmth that mildly pafs away,
Diffolving in the Silence of Decay.

The *Buzzard* not content with equal place,
Invites the feather'd *Nimrods* of his Race,
To hide the thinnefs of their Flock from Sight,
And all together make a feeming, goodly Flight:
But each have fep'rate Int'refts of their own,
Two *Czars*, are one too many for a Throne.
Nor can th' Ufurper long abftain from Food,
Already he has tafted Pigeons Blood:
And may be tempted to his former fare,
When this Indulgent Lord fhall late to Heav'n repair.
Bare benting times, and moulting Months may come,
When lagging late, they cannot reach their home:
Or Rent in Schifm, (for fo their Fate decrees,)
Like the Tumultuous Colledge of the Bees;

They

They fight their Quarrel, by themfelves oppreft ;
The Tyrant fmiles below, and waits the falling feaft.

Thus did the gentle *Hind* her fable end,
Nor would the *Panther* blame it, nor commend ;
But, with affected Yawnings at the clofe,
Seem'd to require her natural repofe.
For now the ftreaky light began to peep ;
And fetting ftars admonifh'd both to fleep.
The Dame withdrew, and, wifhing to her Gueft
The peace of Heav'n, betook her felf to reft.
Ten thoufand Angels on her flumbers waite
With glorious Vifions of her future ftate.

F I N I S.